*You are
cordially invited
to the event
of the year...*

ELLIS LEIGH

Kinship Press

The Gathering Tales
Copyright ©2015 by Ellis Leigh
All rights reserved
ISBN: 978-0-986371-8-8

Kinship Press
P.O. Box 221
kinship press   Prospect heights, IL 60070

For Lisa,
They didn't meet in the wine aisle, but we'll get there.

DAY ONE

killian & lyra

CHAPTER ONE

Lyra

"IF THE WHELP DOESN'T LEARN his place soon, he'll be finding himself alone. I won't put up with such disrespect." My Alpha glared across the room, eyeing the offending wolf with venom in his expression.

I pasted a sympathetic smile on my face and nodded. Playing the part of the good little pack shewolf. Putting on a show for my Alpha so he would believe he was getting the respect he felt he was due. Even though, in my opinion, he was due nothing but a dog pile of angry wolves to force him out of his spot.

I took a sip of my champagne and caught the attention of my packsister, Cheyenne. Her blue eyes twinkled as she rolled them subtly. We weren't fans of our current Alpha. He'd blasted into our pack with talk of becoming more modern and the freedoms we should have. But in the end, he'd become like all the others. Over the summer, he'd kicked out twelve of our unmated packbrothers, claiming they were planning an uprising against him. Everyone knew he did it to cut down on the competition for females. And only days before, he'd called his very first Alpha

Prerogative, demanding three shewolves join him in his bed for mating season: Cheyenne, our packsister Melody, and me.

I gagged every time I thought about what the winter would bring.

The man our Alpha was speaking to looked a bit uncomfortable at the conversation. "Yes, well…we try to promote more modern ways in our pack."

Alpha laughed, loud and quite obviously being sarcastic. "Modern ways get you nothing but trouble." He ran a finger up my arm, dropping his voice to what he considered a sexy tone. "I find I get more from my pack when I enforce strict rules based on the traditional ways. Isn't that right, Lyra?"

I fought off the goose bumps threatening to give away my disgust and nodded once at the other pack leader. "Yes. We appreciate the guidance our Alpha's traditional views bring us and enjoy the structure of our pack."

The old man looked at me with something like pity on his face. I probably deserved such a look, but that didn't make it sting any less. Yes, I was stuck in a pack that thought women were nothing more than objects to be tossed aside and traded for the pleasure of the men. Yes, my Alpha would be demanding my attention in his bed at regular intervals this winter even though I had no interest in him. And yes, my life was not exactly what I'd dreamed about when I was a pup. But being part of what we jokingly called "the Alpha's harem" had gotten me here…to the Gathering. Where wolf shifters from across North America came to meet others and find their fated mates. And while I didn't dare hope I'd be so lucky as to find mine, this was truly my only shot at it. My one chance to escape the man currently making my stomach churn with the lustful way he leered at me.

As soon as the older man excused himself and walked away, Alpha's friendly facade dropped. "Melody, go touch up your makeup. You're looking a bit mussed. Cheyenne, I expect your hand on my waist at all times. And Lyra—" his eyes met mine and a predatory smile spread across his face "—don't drink too much. I think it's high time you and I got to know each other better. You might be spending the night in my room."

I swallowed back the bile rising in my throat. "Of course, Alpha."

Melody's eyes grew wide before she disappeared into the crowd of shifters around us, not that I blamed her. I probably would've done the same had the situation been reversed.

Suddenly, the trumpets played the introduction call. The double doors leading into the ballroom swung open, and a plump man in a formal blue uniform walked in.

"The National Association of the Lycan Brotherhood is pleased to announce the newest pack to our ranks. From far west North Carolina, please welcome the Southern Appalachia pack."

A group of male shifters strode into the ballroom, all tall and muscular, wearing closely tailored suits made of a dark blue fabric. Stunning and strong, they lined the path from the doors toward the dance floor before each one crossed his arms over his impressive chest. Next came a group of equally attractive females, all dressed to the nines in eveningwear. I coveted their long, flowing skirts and more natural faces. Alpha had dressed the three of us to turn men's heads. That meant short, tight dresses, superhigh heels, and more makeup than any woman should wear.

Once the women stood with the men of the pack, the announcer once again raised his voice. "Please welcome this pack to the Brotherhood, and show your honor and respect to their leader—Alpha Killian O'Shea."

I gasped as a man walked into the room. Walked? No, that wasn't the right word. He stalked. A head taller than the rest of his pack, with broad shoulders and thick legs, he ate up the distance from the door to the middle of his pack. Eyes as dark as ebony scanned the room, taking in the various shifters milling about, evaluating them. Determining their worth.

My heart raced and my knees grew weak as he looked my way, devouring me with a single glance. He was a true Alpha, one born with an innate power to lead. I could feel it, sense it even from across the room. A spark ignited within me, one that told me to follow him, to let him lead me, to surrender to him.

My entire body wanted to submit to him.

"He's nothing more than a child."

I nearly hissed at Alpha's denigrating comment, even though I knew he was speaking out of fear. Fear that another wolf was stronger than he. And standing where I was, watching the new Alpha claim the attention of the room even as he kept his eyes on mine, I had no doubt that fear was not unfounded. Killian was quite obviously the biggest, baddest wolf in the room. And I had a deep and all-consuming need to wrap myself around him and never let go.

CHAPTER TWO

"The National Association of the Lycan Brotherhood is pleased to announce the newest pack to our ranks."

"Are you ready for this?" Moira reached up and straightened my tie. I didn't know why she bothered… I'd have the damn thing pulled down again in a matter of minutes.

"As much as I have to be," I growled, brushing her hands away.

"From far west North Carolina, please welcome the Southern Appalachia pack."

The men I'd brought with me for a chance to find their fated mates stormed into the room. I smirked as the gasps and murmurs drifted through the open doorway. We were a new pack to the NALB, but we were hardly weak or green. Our families had been running through the mountains for centuries. We'd just never thought it necessary to participate in these group things. That is, until we went two decades without a single shifter finding their mate.

The men and women of my pack had grown restless and

fearful, so for the first time in our history, I contacted the NALB about joining and attending the Gathering. The packmates I'd brought were some of our older shifters, and I was hopeful at least a few would find mates.

"Easy, killer." Moira grabbed my elbow, stopping me in my tracks. "You'll get out there soon enough." I hadn't even realized I'd been creeping forward. Something was making my wolf anxious, enticing us into the ballroom.

"I hate all this…showbiz stuff."

Moira, my eldest sibling at a mere eleven months older than me, smiled. "You hate everything. I swear, brother dear, if you don't find your mate at this thing, I'm taking you on a countrywide road trip. You're cranky."

I scowled. "I'm not cranky. I'm just worried about the men and women who trust us to lead them."

Moira grew quiet, watching as the women of our pack glided into the ballroom to take their places in line with the men.

"So am I, but I'm worried about you as well." She smiled as I met her gaze. "The men and women of the pack aren't the only ones in need of a mate. Their Alpha could use one as well."

I huffed and returned to staring out the open doorway where I'd be expected to appear shortly. "I can take care of myself."

"Perhaps, but a good woman would do you some good." With a pat to my arm, she followed the women out the door. We'd practiced this ridiculous entrance routine before we left North Carolina, all of us required to know exactly where to be and how to behave. This was the stage show of the NALB, the pomp and circumstance. It was a way of introducing me to the leaders of packs from Canada to Hawaii. This was where we threw off our wolf instincts and pretended to be part of some upper-crust human society. If the NALB was truly looking to support the wolf shifters of North America, this thing would be outside, in the forest, where we belonged. I'd play my part of a well-bred human socialite because my pack needed me to, but I hated every second of it.

When the music changed and the barker announced my name, I strode into the ballroom with as much Alpha power on the surface as I could control. I moved to the center of my pack, eyeing each man and woman surrounding us as they subtly scented the air. I wanted to growl at them all, threaten them in case they dared to think any of us weak, but I reined in my fury. My packmates had so much hope for our future tied up in this event; they'd all be heartbroken if we went home without a single additional pack member. I had to behave. My pack was relying on me.

I studied the shifters in the room, or at least as many as I could see. There had to be hundreds, if not thousands, of shifters on site. All of them looking for a mate, and by the way some of them were sizing me up, looking for a fight as well.

As I passed over a group of men chortling about something probably ridiculously uninteresting, my eyes landed on a woman. One who stared back at me without fear or fury. It'd been a long time since someone, anyone, had been able to hold eye contact with me. The fact that she did it so easily gave me pause and forced me to look a little closer.

Everything about her spoke to me as a man and a wolf— her long, wavy hair, pulled back to show off her porcelain face, wide, deep-set eyes of some indistinguishable light color, the lush curves of her body. She was striking, but it was the scent of her—carried across the distance, blasting its way past other shifters—that struck me as I breathed in.

MATE.

While my wolf howled in delight, the man in me stood tongue-tied and unable to move. Fuck me, I'd come here to find mates for members of my pack, never assuming I'd be lucky enough to find mine as well. But my wolf was certain—the woman staring at me was my fated mate, meant to be mine. And we would do anything to have her.

"Killian? What's wrong?" My sister's whispered concern registered, but I could barely grunt in response.

"Mate."

And then I was off. Stalking my mystery woman. Evaluating her as my prey. Want, need, lust, desire…they all flooded me, making my vision tunnel to only her, my heart beat an erratic rhythm, and my cock harden into steel. I knew the rules of the Gathering, of course. I'd have to be polite and respectful to her Alpha, I'd have to ask him for permission to spend time with her. He had the right to refuse me until the end of the event two days from now, at which point he'd have no more dominion over her. No matter what her Alpha said, she'd be mine at the end of the trip as long as she accepted the mating.

Unfortunately for her Alpha, I was in no mood to play the proper Alpha over the next two days. I wanted her immediately. Beside me, under me, on top of me; I wanted her in my arms *and* my bed. And by the way she was looking back at me, she wanted me as well, which only drove my lust for her higher. I would have her, no matter what her Alpha had to say about it.

The oily fucker standing next to her grabbed her arm as I approached, and my wolf snarled in rage. How dare he touch what was mine? How dare he grab her and treat her so roughly? Given the chance, I'd tear through his hide for even *thinking* he had the right—

"Good evening." Moira appeared in front of me, blocking my path and startling me from my vicious thoughts. "My name is Moira O'Shea, and I'm the NALB liaison for the Appalachia pack. I'd like to introduce my brother, Alpha Killian O'Shea."

Oily Fucker gave me a snake's smile as he extended a hand, keeping one arm around my mate. "Welcome to the NALB. I'm sure you'll find the association helpful while you learn your role as an Alpha."

I'd been staring at my mate, returning her surprised gaze, but his words made my head spin and my lip curl.

"There's nothing to learn. I've been an Alpha for almost a century." I grinned as his smile faltered. Leaning over him, caging him in with my height, I quietly added, "We're new to the NALB, but we're not a new pack. We've been established in the Appalachians since before the Revolutionary War."

"Yes, well…" Oily Fucker looked away, unable to hold my stare. But I didn't give a rat's ass. He meant nothing to me. I only wanted to deal with my mate.

"Hello," I said as her eyes once again met mine.

"Good evening." Her voice was crisp and dry, like an autumn day on the mountain. It fit her and made all my blood rush southward.

I inched closer, taking notice of my sister off to the side, speaking to the oily fucker. At least he no longer had his hands on my mate. Speaking of which…

"You're mine."

I hadn't meant the words to come out so direct, but I couldn't regret it. She had to know we were mates, had to feel the same connection I did.

And if her sultry smile was any indication, she absolutely did.

"Yes, I do believe I am."

A growl rumbled out of my chest, making her eyes go wide. And then she returned the sound. Fuck me, it was so hot. Deep and sensual with a subtle vibration. Her growl made my thoughts go from PG to XXX in a split second. I suddenly wanted to hear that sound while she had her lips around my cock.

"Killian," my sister hissed as she grabbed my elbow. "We have a problem."

"No, we don't." I didn't bother looking away. My mate was smiling at me. Nothing else mattered.

But then my sister yanked on my arm. "Yes, yes, we do."

The other Alpha suddenly appeared next to my mate, grabbing her by the waist and making her stumble. My fingers curled into claws as I righted her, ready to slash into the flesh of the idiot who'd nearly made her fall.

"Your liaison tells me you think you've mated to my shewolf."

I spun and faced the jackass, scowling at his dismissive tone. "I don't think it—I know. She's mine."

His arrogant grin grew as he pulled her away from me. "Not yet, she's not. As her pack Alpha, I have two days before I have to turn her over to you. She's been a good girl for me. I think I might like to give her"—he brushed a curl off her shoulder as she flinched—"a proper goodbye."

My wolf roared even as my sister slammed her shoulder into my chest.

"While we understand the regulations, we'd appreciate any understanding and flexibility you'd be willing to offer. A newly mated Alpha can be very difficult to deal with."

He sneered at both of us before turning away. "No. She's still part of my pack for the next two days. Until then, she does what I say."

I wanted to roar and knock the prick to the ground, but the responsibility to care for my pack held me back. I needed to give my packmates time to mingle and meet people, to sniff out a mate. I'd been at the party for barely ten minutes, and already I was ready to toss aside their chances to find eternal happiness for my own wants and needs. That would not be living up to my title of Alpha.

"Arrogant little fucker," my sister growled low and quiet as she placed a hand on my chest to keep me from chasing my mate. "What now?"

"Now, you find every one of our packmates and tell them they have tonight, and tonight only. They need to spread out and hunt down any potential mates."

"Why?" she asked. "What are you doing to do?"

I grinned as my mate glanced over her shoulder, our eyes meeting for a brief moment before she disappeared in a crowd of people.

"I'm going to do what I do best. Get what I want."

CHAPTER THREE

"Is he looking?"

Cheyenne glanced over my shoulder. "Looking? The man's practically devouring you with his eyes. Good Lord, I can't believe you're mated to him. That's one fine-ass hunk of shifter."

I bit back a grin. "I know."

"Think Alpha will let you go?"

"He has to." I shrugged. "It's just a matter of if he'll let me go tonight, or if he'll force me to stay with him the next two days."

My stomach dropped at the thought of being anywhere near my Alpha's room. It seemed so *wrong*. I'd met my mate, and I would happily scream my acceptance of him if asked. And yet, because of some antiquated law that made me more property than individual, my Alpha could keep us apart for days. Hell, if we'd met on pack property, he could keep us apart for years. I had no idea how those poor wolves managed. Already, I was practically trembling in need of my new mate. I wanted to be by Killian's side, in his arms and his bed…immediately.

But Alpha had told Killian he wanted to keep me for these

next two days, as was his right. And he wanted to give me a proper goodbye. I had no idea what he meant by that, but it made me queasy. Just the thought of touching my Alpha made me feel ill.

Melody, the third packsister brought by the Alpha as his arm candy, weaved her way through the crowd. She'd been gone for quite a long time considering she'd only been refreshing her makeup.

"Where've you been?" Cheyenne asked her.

"The bathrooms are way the heck back there." She turned and pointed. "It took me nearly twenty minutes just to find them."

An idea immediately formed in my head. Maybe, just maybe, I could sneak a little time alone with my mate.

"Come with me," I hissed at Cheyenne.

She raised an eyebrow. "Where?"

I winked and turned to my Alpha, who was busy arguing pack politics with some red-haired man.

"Pardon me, sir." I pulled out my best little girl voice, the one I knew he could never say no to.

He turned, frowning at me for interrupting him. "What is it?"

"I ask permission to use the ladies' room, sir."

His eyes gleamed at my submission. I hated it, wanted to spit the bitter words from my mouth, but it was my one chance. He loved a woman who wouldn't make a decision without his input.

"Yes, well"—he leered, his eyes traveling over the extra-short dress and glittering fishnet stockings he'd chosen for me to wear—"be quick about it. Cheyenne, go with her. Come find me if that so-called Alpha comes sniffing around my girl."

Cheyenne whispered a quiet "Yes, sir" as I nodded, my stomach filling with butterflies at the thought of escaping Alpha, even for a few moments.

As soon as Alpha turned back to his conversation, I pulled Cheyenne's arm and hissed, "Let's go."

"Where?"

"To the bathroom. Just like I told him." I cut a path through the crowd of shifters, pulling Cheyenne behind me. When I was far enough away from Alpha, I glanced behind me to find Killian in the crowd. He stood at the edge of a group of older shifters, watching me with a curious expression on his face. I gave him a smile and nodded my head in the direction of the hallway leading to the restrooms.

Cheyenne huffed as our heels clacked across the dance floor. "I really don't have to go."

"Neither do I. Now, hurry."

CHAPTER FOUR

Killian

FOR WAY TOO LONG, THAT oily fucker paraded *my* mate around the party while I watched from the corner like a chump. He had his arm around her waist, pulling her against his side, touching what was mine. Had we been back home, I'd have killed him already. But I had to rein in those instincts for a little longer. The future of my entire pack lay in our networking with other shifters. Already, the men and women of the Appalachia pack were scouring the building, sniffing out all guests of the Gathering to try to locate a mate. The fact that I'd found mine had given them all hope, and they took my deadline of this evening seriously. There was no way I was going to bed without my mate beside me.

"You'd better calm that growl, Killian. Someone's going to think you're a little pissed."

I grunted a laugh as my sister moved to stand next to me. "A little pissed doesn't even begin to describe it."

From across the room, my mate tossed a glance over her shoulder as she moved away from me, her eyes meeting with mine. It was a gut-punch kind of moment, one where all this emotion—desire, lust, affection, need—coiled up inside of me and exploded through my body. She'd been doing that a lot, catching my eye. Perhaps it was because she felt my stare. Or maybe she ached for me the same way I did for her.

"Where's she going?"

My sister glanced her way. "Looks like she's headed to the restroom."

I grunted an agreement as my mate gave me a smile and seemed to nod her head at something, though what, I couldn't figure out.

"You know," my sister said, keeping her voice light and quiet, "the ladies' room here is very inconvenient. It took me a while just to find it, and then it was down this long, dark, lonesome hallway lined with all these empty conference rooms. People could get lost."

I felt the furrow of my brow as I watched my mate disappear to the other side of the hall. "And I need to know this because?"

My sister huffed. "Because it appears the object of your obsession is headed that way. If you hurry and aren't obvious about it, you might be able to sneak a few minutes alone with her. At least give her a proper introduction."

I whipped my head in her direction. "Where?"

She smiled and nodded her head in the direction my mate had just gone. "There. Back wall, hall on the right, keep following it past all the turns."

I was striding across the room before the last word rolled off her tongue. "Love you, sis," I called over my shoulder. I could barely hear her laughing as I cut through the mass of people in my way. This was it, my chance. I just wanted to make sure she was okay, introduce myself properly, and maybe figure out a way to get her away from her Alpha. As long as she wanted me to, that is.

I turned the corner as my sister said and followed the

seemingly endless hallway around half a dozen turns. It was like a fucking maze. The scent of my mate hung heavy in the air, making my wolf anxious. Soon. A few more doors. A final turn and—

There she was. Standing in front of a door on the left with her packmate by her side. My mate's eyes went wide when she saw me, and those kissable lips of hers turned up at the corners.

"Well, hello," she said. "Fancy meeting you here."

"Hello." I stopped in front of her, dying to reach for her hand but unsure if my touch would be welcomed. "I wanted to introduce myself properly."

The other woman glanced from one of us to the other with a smile on her face. "I can probably get you about fifteen minutes, but then Alpha's going to get suspicious."

My mate looked her way. "Thank you. I won't be long."

As the woman walked into the ladies' room, my mate nodded her head farther down the hall. "Should we find a quiet spot to talk?"

"That sounds perfect." I led her down the hall a few doors, resting my hand on the curve of her lower back the entire way. The way her muscles flexed under her ridiculously tight black dress made my fingers itch for more contact, but I held back. Kept my composure. Played the gentleman.

But the second the door closed behind us, my mate spun and wrapped herself around me, her lips crashing into mine.

"Fuck me." I ran both hands down to her ass, cupping and pulling her against my straining cock as I slid my tongue inside. Damn, she tasted good.

"No time," she mumbled, clutching my shoulders and biting my lower lip. Hard.

I growled as I owned her mouth. This kiss wasn't sweet or introductory. There was no single bit of affection in it. This was pure carnal need on display. And it was perfect.

"I swear, I was just going to introduce myself." My hands

slid lower, finding the straps of the silky thing holding up the sparkly stockings covering those long legs of hers. I groaned and yanked her closer as my fingers danced along uncovered flesh, my lips and tongue still working with hers.

"You're Killian, we're mated, and that asshole Alpha of mine is trying to keep us apart. Anything else I need to know?" She yanked me backward, not stopping until we reached a conference table. Still not breaking the kiss, she slid onto the table and spread her legs around my hips.

"Nope. Not a goddamned thing." I happily pressed against her. Fucking her mouth, pushing her dress up around her hips. "You're the sexiest thing I've ever seen."

She grinned and licked her way up my neck, over my jawline to my ear, whispering to me, "I've been wet since the moment you walked in the ballroom."

I growled and dragged my fingers up the inside of her thighs. "Can you be quiet?" My fingers quickly found where she was hot and swollen. Fuck me, the woman didn't have anything on under her dress but those hot-as-fuck little strappy things and the sheer fabric on her legs. So sexy.

She met my eyes and nodded as I traced a knuckle along the edge of her pussy. Just a light touch…a tease. But then she groaned, and there was no more time for teasing. The woman had been driving me mad since I first saw her, and I wanted to make her just as crazy for me.

"Lean back a little."

She did as I asked, licking her lips and spreading her legs even wider. Dress hiked up, lips swollen from our kisses, gorgeous pink pussy on display… She was a debauched angel, ready for me to catch her as she fell.

"Are you real?" The words escaped me without intention or forethought. My mate tilted her head, a small smile coming to her face as she watched me.

"Very much so, and I've been waiting to find you for a long

time."

I growled while I slid one finger inside her, finding her hot and wet. Working her clit with my thumb, I pumped in and out a few times. Learning her tells, beginning the long journey to find all the secret spots that would make her tremble from my touch. Twisting and sliding my fingers inside her, I watched as her breathing increased, her skin flushed, and her body began to shake.

"What's your name, beautiful?" I increased my pace, already feeling the flutters of an impending orgasm from within her. "Tell me who I'm blessed to call mate."

Her head fell back as I added a third finger and pressed a little harder with my thumb.

"Oh, yes," she breathed, her body arching. "I'm Lyra of the Bloodstone pack. Please…fuck, please."

"I've got you, sweet girl." I bent over her, my fingers buried deep inside as I searched out her mouth. Lapped at her lips. Matched the way my tongue met hers with the rhythm of my hand below.

She practically jumped off the table when I curled my fingers, stroking her from within, increasing my tempo and pressure. "You're going to make me come."

I growled as her eyes—gray like a stormy sky—met mine. "That's the whole idea."

She clutched and writhed, riding my hand for all it was worth. Fuck, I wanted it to be my cock inside of her. Wanted to feel her wrapped all around me as I thrust into her. But this would have to do. A moment, a brief interlude, but at least I could make sure she knew who owned her pussy from this point forward. I could make sure my mate found satisfaction at my hand.

Three more thrusts and her body clamped down, her thighs shaking and her head thrown back.

"Yes…yes…yes." Breathy chants left her lips as I continued

to work her, making it last, keeping her in the moment for as long as I could. My hand still inside her, milking her orgasm from her body, I licked a line from her chin to her ear. "I'm your fucking mate. This?" I cupped her pussy as my fingers pressed deep inside her, making her moan and shiver from the pressure of my palm against her swollen and sensitive clit. "This is mine now."

She nodded against my chest, her breath still coming in pants. "I know. Hopefully, my Alpha will come to his senses and let me join you tonight instead of making us wait."

I grinned as her eyes met mine, pulling my fingers from her pussy and bringing them to my lips. I licked and lapped the digits, loving the way her eyes widened. The renewed lust I saw growing there. "Doesn't fucking matter what the oily fucker says. The only person whose opinion matters is you. As long as you accept me as your mate, you'll be in my bed tonight and every night from this moment on."

A warm, slow smile spread across her face. "I accept you, Killian O'Shea. In my bed, in my heart, and in my life."

I leaned over her, kissing her hard and deep as I gripped her hips. "Then you're mine, and nothing that little pissant says can stop me from having you tonight."

CHAPTER FIVE

WITH THE TASTE OF KILLIAN'S kiss still on my lips, I slipped out of our little corner of the Gathering and down the hall toward the ballroom. My knees were still wobbly, my thighs still wet from our time together, but I had a job to do. If I had any shot of getting away from Alpha before the end of the night, I'd need to play the perfect little harem girl for him.

After a quick stop in the bathroom to wash up, I reapplied my lipstick, refastened my ponytail, and strode into the ballroom as if I owned it. Killian had already taught me something—it was all in the entrance.

"Lyra, there you are." Alpha may have been trying to look the ever-patient and understanding shifter, but I knew him better than that. He was pissed, and I would pay a price tonight for my disappearing if whatever Killian had planned fell through. Still, my time with my new mate was totally worth it. My body was still tingling from the way he'd worked me over.

I kept my head up as I approached, spying Killian's sister by Alpha's side. "I apologize for taking so long, Alpha. I was touching up my makeup and lost track of time."

He pulled me into his side, wrapping his arm around me and grabbing my hip until I nearly squealed in pain.

"Yes, well. Next time, do try to be quicker about it." He sniffed, his nostrils flaring as he glared at me. I kept my head up and my back straight, refusing to give him a single ounce of ammunition against me.

"Shall we proceed to dinner?" Moira asked, interrupting our stare-down.

I nodded once and stepped out of Alpha's hold. We all moved toward the dining tables at the back of the room. And by all, I meant Killian's sister as well as our pack. Though there was no sign of my new mate.

"I'm so glad the staff placed us at your table," Moira said as we reached our assigned place. Each plate had a small card centered on it with a name on the front in fancy script. I walked around the table searching for mine, nearly grinning when I saw that Killian and I would be sitting next to each other. Moira and Cheyenne flanked my Alpha, who was seated all the way across the table from me. Melody sat to my left, one more barrier between Alpha and me. It was my lucky night.

"Allow me." Killian swooped in as I reached for my chair, smiling kindly as I nodded my thanks.

"Why, thank you." I settled in my seat and placed my napkin in my lap.

Before he moved into his own seat, Killian leaned over my right shoulder and whispered, "You're positively stunning when you smile."

I nearly blushed, hiding my smile behind my napkin as he took his seat. He pulled his chair close, angling his body, resting his thigh against mine but keeping our shoulders apart. Looking to all the world like two strangers sitting next to one another… as long as the viewers didn't lift the tablecloth.

Alpha glared at me from his side of the table. "This can't

possibly be right. The event organizers wouldn't break up packs when they arranged the seating."

Moira smiled and glanced around the room. "It appears that's exactly what they did. I see my packmates at a number of different tables. Perhaps they're hoping for more mingling this way."

Alpha snorted. "Mingling? Is that what you call it? Because really, the Gathering has become nothing more than a glorified orgy. All these worthless wolves claiming to have found their mates." He looked right at Killian. "I have a good mind to take my women and head home tonight. Keep them from having to witness the debauchery that will begin once a little more wine has been consumed."

Killian growled and moved to stand, but I stopped him with a hand on his stomach. If Alpha went through with his threat, he could stop Killian and me from being together for months or even years. Our only chance for a quick mating was to not anger Alpha, to stay at the Gathering, and to get through the next two days with as little strife as possible.

Moira's eyes darted our way, checking on Killian before she leaned closer to Alpha. "I can't say I've seen any…debauchery just yet. I think I'll stick around." She moved back, giving him a seductive smile. "I might learn something."

Alpha's eyes were round, his lips parted as he took a great gulp of air. Well, well, someone was a little aroused by the petite woman. Moira tossed a quick glance my way, giving me a wink before returning her attention to my Alpha. Killian growled low in his throat as he watched Alpha lean into his sister's space and begin whispering to her.

"Hush," I admonished quietly. "She's pretending."

Killian grunted. "He's not."

I placed my hand on his thigh and leaned toward him, keeping my voice as low as I could. "No, but he's distracted by her. I, for one, am greatly appreciative of her subterfuge."

Killian didn't answer; in fact, he'd gone completely still. When I looked up, his gaze burned into mine. He looked at me as if I were some kind of delectable treat and he hadn't eaten in days. I didn't know what was making him stare at me like that until I felt a muscle in his thigh jump. Oh, that was *so* not his thigh.

My hand had moved of its own volition and was currently resting with my fingertips brushing his very hard cock. I let out a breath and flexed my hand, still staring into his dark eyes. His growl rumbled deep and quiet from his chest as I smiled at him. And then I wrapped my fingers around him through the fabric of his suit pants.

"You'll unman me," he whispered.

I smiled as sweetly as I could, thankful for the empty seats on the other side of him. "That's the plan."

With no hesitation or fear, I unzipped his fly and slipped my hand inside. And then I raised an eyebrow as I immediately met warm, soft skin.

He chuckled and shrugged. "Apparently we both had the same idea."

I shook my head and fought back a laugh as he leaned forward.

His eyes stayed on mine, a seductive smirk on his pouty lips. "Though my lack of undergarments is more habit than a one-night thing. I prefer to be unencumbered."

I raised an eyebrow. "Maybe you should teach me the benefits of being...unencumbered."

"Anytime, beautiful."

Running my fingers up his length, I worked my hand farther inside so I could get a better grip. I was wrapping my hand around him when—

"Would you care for more bisque?"

I jumped as a waiter in a black tuxedo appeared next to me. "Pardon?"

Killian held my wrist in place, refusing to let me pull away. "We're fine, thank you."

The waiter nodded and hurried to the next group at the table, apparently none the wiser.

"That was close," I mumbled.

"No, it really wasn't. But if you keep going, I promise not to take too long." Killian's grin disarmed me, making my heart warm and my smile appear out of nowhere.

I leaned in, just enough to brush my cheek on his shoulder and whisper, "Take your time."

He jerked as I gripped him, this time strong and direct. I adjusted the tablecloth to make sure no one could see what I was doing and inched closer. And then I pumped my hand up and down his shaft, gripping him, squeezing and twisting as I went.

I rolled my fingers over the head, spreading his pre-come as he hissed. I loved the sound, wanted to hear him do it again. Soon, I was stroking him as much as I could while trying to keep my upper body still. Loving how hard and yet soft he felt, cherishing every small groan and growl. Wishing I could crawl under the table to wrap my mouth around him. I kept my hand moving over his long, thick cock as all around us, shifters slurped their soup obliviously and made small talk. And while I smiled at my Alpha.

CHAPTER SIX

killian

FUCK ME, HER HAND—HER hot, smooth, little hand—was wrapped around my cock. Working me. Making me feel so good. I wanted to come, wanted to blow my load right then and there, but I hated the thought of her stopping. I wanted more, needed it in a way I'd never experienced. Every second of her skin on mine was a damned gift, and I was going to take my time with it.

Her fingers spread over my head before sliding down again, and I fought every instinct not to roll my eyes at the pleasure shooting up my spine. She was going to make me come. And soon. Right here in a room full of people, with a man who smelled like stale cigarettes a mere six feet away. But fuck, I didn't care. I'd stand up and flash the entire room if it meant she'd keep touching me. Keep pumping me. Keep teasing my slit with the edge of her thumb.

"Holy shit." I bit my lip as she sped up, her grip strengthening around me. "Now."

I swear she smiled smugly as I came all over her hand, doing everything in my power not to make a fucking sound. I wanted to groan and thrust into her tight little fist, but I held still, barely shifting my hips as she eased her grip. Still, the orgasm rocked me. Tingles shot from my balls all the way up my spine, ricocheting in my head before heading back down to quiver in the tip of my dick. Never had a simple hand job felt so good.

"Better?" She gave me a wicked smile, one filled with pure feminine pride. Yeah, okay…she made me come like a high schooler in a matter of minutes. I'd give her that one.

"Fuck yes." I coughed and tried to act as if nothing was going on as Moira and the oily fucker glanced across the table. Once their attention was back on—well, each other—I leaned in to whisper in Lyra's ear.

"I need to go clean up. Will you be okay by yourself for a few minutes?"

She shrugged, her eyes flitting to her Alpha. "Yes, of course."

I didn't want to leave her. I wanted to drag her with me and give her my claiming bite right then in front of all the shifters in the room, but I knew I needed to behave. For how much longer I'd be able to, though, I had no idea. My wolf was positively starving for our new mate.

"If he gives you any trouble," I whispered as I stood up, "just get my sister's attention. She'll make sure he doesn't step out of line."

Lyra rolled her eyes, dismissing me as she subtly used her napkin to wipe off her hand. "Really, I'll be fine."

She may have been able to play off her emotions with others, but not me. I was her mate. I could practically smell the anxiety pouring off her.

I squeezed her shoulder, forcing her to meet my gaze once more. "Two minutes."

"Go." She smiled, small and not reaching her eyes, but a smile nonetheless. Unfortunately, her Alpha called her right then, and even that sad excuse for a smile fell. "Hurry back."

◊ ◊ ◊

After the fastest piss known to man and a quick hand-wash, I rushed back to the ballroom. A few hours left to deal with this bullshit, and then I could be alone with my mate. Fuck her Alpha; she was coming back to my room tonight. If I had to throw her on the table and bite her in front of all these people, I would.

Making the final turn toward my table, I quickened my step to get back to Lyra, but her chair was empty. I glanced across the table only to see my mate sitting on the lap of her Alpha. And not looking too thrilled about it. My growl rumbled deep in my chest, warning all those around that my wolf was on a short leash. Most of the people I passed moved away, looking nervous. As they should have been. My wolf was ready to explode.

But then the oily fucker grabbed Lyra's chin and turned her face roughly. Moira stood from her chair, tugging on his arm, but the idiot apparently had a death wish. He shoved my sister back as he pressed his lips to Lyra's.

The room turned red as I roared. That fucker was dead. Lyra was my mate. Mine. And she wanted to be with me. How dare he disrespect me by touching what he knew I would be claiming? Hell no. The man was done. Fuck this whole group of backward shifters; I was taking my woman and bringing her home to the mountains where I could love her, spoil her, and treat her the way a woman deserved to be treated.

I stalked the rest of the way across the room, not even paying attention as my sister stood and called my name. This situation was past the point of niceties and politics. Lyra was mine. Done.

"Ah, young one. Come and sit. See what a real Alpha gets from—"

He never had a chance to finish his sentence. As soon as I reached them, I grabbed Lyra by the waist and hoisted her up and over my shoulder. When her Alpha stood as if to take her from me, I swung. His face made a satisfying crunch as it connected with my fist.

"Killian!" Lyra's yell made me pause, mere feet from where her Alpha lay sprawled on the ballroom floor.

"Do you want to stay with him?" My question came out on a growl, my chest heaving with the effort to hold back my rage.

Lyra barely paused before answering. "No."

"Do you want to come with me?"

This time, her answer was immediate and strong. "Yes."

"Good." With nothing left to say, I spun and strode toward the ballroom doors. The crowd parted as I passed, no one seeming to want to get in my way. They were smart. Two men in what looked like security uniforms stepped in front of me before I could leave, though.

"Is there a problem here?" the one on the left asked, glancing at Lyra as she lay across my shoulder.

"She's my mate, and she's accepted me as such." I glared at the two men as a snarl curled my lip. I could feel the fur growing through my skin, knew I was partial-shifting right there in the ballroom, but I didn't care. "We have no problem. Do you?"

The one on the left looked shocked and a little scared, but the one on the right was focused on Lyra. "Are you okay, ma'am?"

"Yes, for God's sake, yes." Her hands slapped down on my back as she huffed and kicked. "Just let him leave with me so I can stop flashing the whole damn room."

I grinned and smacked her on the ass. "See? We're all good."

And with that, we walked out the doors and to the stairs. Fuck the elevator; I couldn't wait to get my woman alone.

CHAPTER SEVEN

Lyra

I WAS GIGGLING BY THE time Killian climbed three flights of stairs and found what I assumed was his room down one of the endless hallways.

"Laugh all you want now"—he threw open the door and carried me over the threshold—"because in a few minutes"—he slammed and locked the door—"you won't be able to."

He pulled me down, pressing me against the closed door with his big body. For the love of the gods, the man was beyond strong. He wasn't even winded from the trek. I wrapped my legs around his hips, pressing my soaking wet pussy against the hard bulge in his pants and smiling as seductively as I could.

"And what exactly are you going to do to me to make me stop laughing, Alpha O'Shea?"

Instead of joking back, his face grew serious, his dark eyes locking on mine.

"I'm not like him, you know." He sighed when I gave him a confused look. "I won't force you to do anything. I wanted you away from him, and I want you in my bed, but I won't force you."

"I know," I whispered as I ran a single finger down the side of his face. "You're my mate. I accept you, I honor that bond, and I give myself to you fully."

He sighed and closed his eyes for a brief moment. "Oh, thank fuck, because I want you wrapped around my cock so bad that the whole no forcing you thing might have been a challenge."

I smiled for a single second before his mouth met mine, his tongue pressing through my lips to stroke my own. Damn, he tasted good. Like whiskey and honey; bitter and sweet.

The kiss turned hotter, our bodies responding to the arousal growing between us. As his lips moved to my neck, I suckled his earlobe, grazing it with my teeth as I writhed against him.

"Fuck, Lyra. You'd better quit or else we won't even make it to the bed."

I groaned at the dirty images his words created for me. He was so strong, so muscular and big; there was no doubt he could push, pull, hold, and twist me into any number of positions. And I wanted him to. I wanted him to so much. I gripped his shoulders and arched into him as I whispered, "Who needs a bed?"

He growled deep and low, his hands squeezing my ass. "I'd hoped to make our first time special or some such shit."

I moaned as he thrust his hips into mine, his hard cock pressing against my clit in the most delicious way. "As long as we end up with your dick inside me, that'll be special enough."

He grinned, giving my chin a nip. "Jesus, you're fucking perfect."

One hand left my ass so he could unzip his pants. He grunted and shook, obviously trying to release his dick as he held me up. I continued licking, sucking, and biting my way up and down his neck, to his ear, across his jaw. I couldn't get enough of him. Needed to taste as much of his skin as I could.

Finally, his hand returned to my ass, this time his fingers spreading to trail over the curve and down along the sides of my pussy. I gasped and groaned as one errant middle finger slid between my cheeks to press against my ass.

"That we'll do later," he murmured as he pushed me up the wall a little higher. He forced my legs a little wider, the head of his cock resting exactly where I wanted it. "Right now, you're fucking soaked, and I plan to take full advantage of that."

With no more than a grunt and a kiss to my lips, he pushed inside me. I gasped and dropped my head to his shoulder, completely amazed at how good he felt. How big. How much the stretch of my walls around him turned me on.

"Tight. So hot and tight." His whispered declarations were followed by a slow withdrawal from my pussy before he once again thrust his way inside. Deeper this time. Harder. "Fuck, baby. Your pussy was made for me. So hot and wet. So tight around my cock."

I groaned and bit his shoulder. Not hard enough to draw blood, not a full mating bite, but enough to make him shiver and curse. He increased the tempo of his thrusts, growling and cursing as he fucked me right there against the wall. My dress was hiked up above my hips, my stockings and heels still on, but I didn't care. I loved that he wanted me so much, he couldn't wait. Loved that his lust for me was that strong.

"Fuck, not gonna last." His fingers slid around to where we were joined, adding another layer of sensation to our coupling. I moaned and shook as one long finger reached around to my clit, circling the flesh in time with his thrusts. His finger pressing on my clit, his thick cock inside me, I came without warning and with a yelp that probably alerted the entire floor to what we were doing. Killian followed soon after, grinding his teeth and snarling as he released inside me, his muscles hard and his body wound tight.

"Jesus, baby," he whispered, panting against my shoulder.

I chuckled as my feet dropped to the ground. "That's one way to end the night."

He huffed a laugh as he pulled me against him, claiming my mouth in a brutal kiss before whispering, "End it? Fuck that… We're just getting started."

With a wicked glint in his eyes but gentle hands, he stripped off my dress and removed my heels. On his knees, he brought his hands up to my garter straps, running his palms along my legs the whole way.

"Do you have any idea how fucking sexy these are on you?"

I shook my head, watching him. Unable to look away as he stared at my thighs.

"The dress can go; I'll never make you wear something you're not comfortable with in public. But these?" His finger slid under one of the straps, pulling on the elastic and silk. "I want you in these every time we have to go to some stupid dress-up function. I want to see you all polished and elegant but know, underneath, my girl's completely naughty and ready for me." He leaned forward to press a soft kiss against my bare mound. "Just the thought of you in these tempting little stocking things was making me hard all night. I couldn't bear to let you out of my sight."

I ran a hand through his hair. "Then we can leave them on."

He glanced up at me, looking as if I'd just given him the best gift. "Really?"

"Sure. If it gets you to look at me like that, I'll wear them every day for you."

He groaned, stretching out his tongue to lick a line along my swollen clit. "Fuck me, you really are perfect."

Before I could respond, he stood and yanked his shirt over his head. Within seconds, he was completely naked, standing before me like some kind of gorgeous statue. Muscular, with thick, black hair over his chest and leading down to a line trailing straight to his cock, he was the full definition of man.

Strong, powerful, intense.

"Come." His command was quiet but filled with Alpha power. I followed without hesitation, never looking away from those amazing black eyes. "I want you on your back."

He directed me onto the mattress. I ended up with my head on a pillow, my legs bent at the knee and spread for him. Blatant. His hand was wrapped around his hard cock, stroking himself as he stared at me.

"Prettiest fucking pussy I've ever seen," he said, right before he grabbed my thighs and buried his face in me. I shouted a curse as I struggled to keep my body from rocking backward, his aggressive tonguing of my clit making my thighs tremble in his hands.

"Please," I whimpered, feeling empty, needing something more than his mouth on me.

"Please what?" he whispered against me. "Tell me what you need."

"Please fuck me. I need your cock. Please." I twisted as he leaned back, rolling to my knees. Glancing back at him, I dropped my shoulders and made sure my ass was in the air. Making myself available to him however he wanted me.

He froze for about three seconds, his growl growing louder as his hands kneaded my thighs.

"Whatever you need, baby. I'll give you anything." He climbed onto the bed behind me, spreading my knees farther with his own.

"Just you," I hissed, groaning as he slid inside me, the angle making the sensation more intense than our first coupling. Hand on my neck, holding me down, he pounded into me, setting a furious pace that pushed me up the bed and made my knees burn. But I loved it. Loved how roughly he handled me, even though his hands were gentle. Loved this huge, strong man fucking me like he owned me, even as he let me twist and beg and tell him more or less what to do. Perfect. He was so fucking perfect.

"Aw, fuck," he grunted as his thrusts lost their rhythm. "Want you to be mine. Just mine. Forever."

"Yes." I howled as my walls tightened and fluttered, my stomach burning with the rush of my oncoming orgasm. "Make me yours."

His growl turned to a roar. He yanked my hair, pulling me back against his body as he shook and thrust and kept his dick seated deep inside me. And when he came, when he wrapped an arm around my shoulders and pinned my back to his chest, he dropped his head to my shoulder and bit the flesh curving up to my neck. Claiming me forever as his.

I came around his cock, screaming with the intensity of his claiming bite. The power of his wolf surged through me, bringing me more pleasure that I'd ever known. Over and over, waves of pleasure rocked my body, never easing up, seemingly endless as he held me with his arms and bite. As he pumped into me. Until finally, with a groan and final shiver of delight, he pulled his teeth from my neck and licked the wound.

"Mine...forever."

CHAPTER EIGHT

SHE WAS LAUGHING AGAIN. Not that I blamed her. I'd been licking her neck and pinching her nipples for a good ten minutes while I growled in a way she said sounded like a purr. But wolves didn't fucking purr.

Still, I didn't mind the giggle or the way her plump ass wiggled against my cock as the room began to glow with the dawn. I'd been inside of her at least five times over the course of the night, and I was definitely ready to go again. I'd probably always be ready for her.

But when I wrapped my arms around her and slid my hands over her hipbones, she twisted away.

"C'mon, handsome," she said as she stood from the bed, not the least bit shy about standing naked in front of me. "I want to take care of you this time."

"Pretty sure you took care of me a few times already tonight," I said as I reached for her. She dodged my hands and headed for the bathroom.

"I'm taking a shower. You can either join me under the steamy water, where I promise to take extra special care of you—" she turned and gave me one hell of a wicked smirk"—or you can stay out here by yourself and rest. I'll be back in a few minutes, and we can just go to sleep if you like."

I waited a whole four seconds before I bounded out of bed and chased her into the bathroom. She turned the taps on as I came up behind her, my hands going unerringly to her hips. I rubbed myself against her ass, nipping her neck and wrapping my arms around to palm her heavy breasts.

"Glad you could make it." Her voice was teasing, and I loved it. Loved that she felt that comfortable with me already.

I nipped her neck, giving her a good strong growl in the process. "Like I'd give up a chance to see you wet."

She stepped into the shower, pulling me with her. "You've seen parts of me wet already."

The hot water flowed between us, the steam rising fast. "I'm willing to see whatever you want to show me, naughty girl."

She growled soft and low as she pulled me closer. "Just for you."

"Good." I pushed her wet hair off her face and leaned over to press my mouth to hers. I loved kissing this woman. The way her plump lips fitted to mine, how her tongue stroked so seductively, the breathy little moans and gasps she made. Loved it. Couldn't get enough. But apparently she had a different idea.

She kissed over my chin and down my neck. Spent a few minutes laving my collarbone, then a little longer focusing on my nipples. I kept my hands in her hair, not leading her, just holding on. Letting her decide where to go.

Her hands slid over my hips and down my thighs as she dropped to her knees. I nearly came right there, just looking at her like that. Wet, needy, hungrily staring at my cock as it bobbed in front of her. Fuck, I wanted her mouth on me. Wanted it more than just about anything at that moment.

"The women of my pack like to talk," she whispered, her

hand circling my cock and stroking me from base to tip. "One of the things they share is where they gave their claiming mark to their mates. Some are like you, putting it in a spot that's obvious and apparent to anyone."

She was pure sex, all seduction and need. Still teasing my cock, her other hand came up to trace the bite mark I'd left on her shoulder. I growled when she touched it, loving the way it glowed red against her pale skin. The way my mark looked on her skin.

"But some of the women prefer more intimate locations." She leaned forward and licked the head of my cock, making me shiver. "Over the heart, the hip, the thigh. Their mates see it as a badge of honor, to have that mark in a place that meant the woman was so obviously in a submissive position when she gave it." She looked up at me, drops of water like crystals on her eyelashes. "Where do you want my bite, mate?"

I blew out a deep breath, my cock practically leaking as she went back to licking the head. "I'm all yours," I whispered. "Do what you wish."

She grinned. "I was hoping you'd say that."

Leaning forward, she took me all the way into her mouth. I growled and fell back against the wall, the sudden heat and pressure making my knees wobble. She sucked and licked and teased like no other, bringing me to the edge of orgasm time and again before pulling back, driving me absolutely crazy. And when she did it again, when I thought for sure she was going to kill me with her teasing, she slipped a hand up to my balls and pulled, rolled, massaged. I came with a snarl, her name a prayer on my lips.

But then her mouth left me and her teeth were suddenly deep in my upper thigh. Mere inches from my cock. I hollered a curse and fought to stay on my feet as she bit harder, the force of her wolf causing me to come a second time. Nearly taking me to my knees.

Mine mine mine.

The words reverberated in my head as my wolf howled his pride. Our mate had chosen us, had given herself to us. Our mate had claimed us.

"Jesus fuck." I huffed and panted as she released my skin, lapping at the mark before rubbing her hands all over my thighs, abs, and the base of my dick. "Fucking hell, woman. I thought you were going to kill me."

She laughed as I pulled her to her feet and wrapped my arms around her. We stood that way for what could have been hours, simply holding one another in the warmth of the shower.

"We're mated." Her surprised whisper was barely audible over the sound of the water hitting the shower floor.

"We sure the hell are." I pulled back, looking down at her seriously. "Think you'll like the mountains of North Carolina? Because as much as I know it's your decision, I can't leave my pack. And I refuse to submit to that oily fucker you called Alpha."

She gave me a smile. "I choose to go where you do. Location matters nothing to me."

"Thank fuck." I pressed my lips to hers, kissing her softly. I was about to pick her up and go for wall sex round two when a loud banging sounded through the room. She stiffened in my arms, a look of panic crossing her face.

"Oh God, it's probably Alpha."

"Hush, baby." I turned off the taps and smoothed her hair. "He can't do anything to us. We're fully mated now. Whether we followed his wishes or not, these marks supersede whatever power he claims to have over you."

"But what if you get in trouble?"

"For what? Claiming my mate? So be it. I still got what I came for, even if I did have to break a few rules along the way." I yanked her against me, kissing her until she was breathless before I released her lips. "You are worth every possible sanction they can throw at me."

I wrapped her in one of the fluffy white robes hanging from a hook by the shower and fastened a towel around my hips before stalking toward the door. When I opened it, Moira, our packmate Gideon, a pissed-off looking Oily Fucker, and three regional heads of the NALB stood in the hallway.

"What's this? Have y'all come to celebrate my mating?" I leaned against the doorframe, refusing to let their glares rattle me.

"I've come for Lyra. I did not give my permission for you to take her early."

"Sorry, man, no can do. We've already exchanged mating bites." I shrugged and gave the regional heads my best charm-the-teacher grin. "You know how it is when you meet your mate. Resisting is near impossible."

"Yes, well—"

"Lyra! Get out here right now." Oily Fucker stepped as if to walk past me, but I stopped him with a hand to his chest and a deep growl.

"Don't even fucking think about it."

Before he could reply, Lyra slid up beside me, looking at the men nervously. Her ex-Alpha's eyes immediately went to the red bite mark on her neck, and his face practically turned purple.

"You bit her," he hissed.

"I told you we exchanged mating bites. What'd you expect?"

He looked me over, an arrogant expression growing on his face. "You bit her, but I see no reciprocal bite. If you claimed her against her will, there *will* be hell to pay."

I gripped the ignorant fuck by the throat, yanking him up so he could look me in the eye. "Unlike you, I don't need to force women into my bed."

"Killian didn't claim me against my will." Lyra took a step forward, anger burning in her eyes as she placed her hand on my arm. Trying to calm me, I knew. I set the man who'd once lorded his power over her back on his feet, growling the whole time. "Our claiming was mutual. There's no crime here."

Oily Fucker straightened the wrinkles in his shirt, looking affronted and a bit less sure of himself. "Then where's his bite? I see no mark on him."

She blushed and glanced at me. The NALB guys looked over my chest and arms, giving me a sour frown when they saw no mark. But I just grinned.

And dropped my towel.

"My bite's right here." I gripped my junk and moved it to the side to show off Lyra's teeth marks. "Happy now?"

The Alpha blanched, turning away after he got a good eyeful of my cock. The regional heads each nodded, looking as if they were fighting to keep from laughing.

"Sorry to disturb you, Alpha O'Shea. Congratulations on your mating."

"Thank you. But if y'all will excuse us, I have a mate who should be screaming my name right now." I slammed the door in their faces, pulling Lyra into my arms.

"I say we celebrate." I picked her up and carried her to the bed, tossing her on the mattress.

She giggled as she bounced. "What exactly did you have in mind?"

Grinning, I spread her legs wide and crawled over her, stopping when my cock pressed against her. "Anything you want. For as long as you want."

"Forever?"

My growl was loud, filled with pride and happiness. With a shift of my hips, I slid inside, the heat of her making me shiver as I seated myself good and deep.

"Yes, forever."

Day Two

gideon & kalie

CHAPTER ONE

"My bite's right here. Happy now?"

I fought back a grin as Alpha Killian stood in the hall, bold as brass with his hand gripping his dick. The man had a backbone of steel. The officials who'd come to bring some kind of complaint against Killian chattered a bit more, but my attention was already gone. My entire body felt itchy with the need to shift and run. To let my wolf lead me, even if only for a few moments.

"Gideon?"

I turned at Moira's voice, meeting her dark eyes. "Yes, ma'am?"

The look of concern on her face turned into a soft smile. "You seem a little anxious."

"Yes, well"—I fought back a growl as I ran a hand through my hair—"these suits and their rules make me want to challenge one of them to a real fight."

She placed a hand on my arm. "We're not here to get into fights. Everyone knows you're a strong wolf, Gideon. Hell, they can see it. You're almost as big as Killian. But we're here to find mates, and fighting won't help us do that."

Something that felt a lot like shame burned in my gut. I hated admitting a weakness to anyone, especially someone in a position of power over me like Moira, but she was kind and caring. She would never betray me by exploiting my weakness.

"I'm beginning to think my mate's not here," I said, keeping my voice low and quiet.

Moira frowned a little. "You've been here less than a day. Now that we know Killian's antics didn't get us kicked out, we have two full days to mingle and meet people. Don't give up just yet. Things of value take time to nurture." She ran her fingers down my bicep, over the curve of my elbow, along the muscles and veins of my forearm. I'd spent years building my strength, fighting side by side with Alpha Killian even before he'd taken the title. Moira's action was one of respect—she was reminding me of that strength. Of how worthy I was of finding a mate.

"I'm trying." I eyed the exit sign at the end of the hall, fighting my own body at the need to go for a run. I couldn't leave just yet, though. Moira'd asked for my assistance, and until she released me, I had to stay with her. She was a leader in the pack, and Killian would—

"Go."

I jerked and turned to face her, afraid I'd misheard. "Pardon?"

"Go." She shooed me toward the exit. "Get out there and find your mate. I have high hopes for you, Gideon."

"You're a goddess, Miss Moira." I grinned as I hurried backward down the hall.

"Yeah, yeah, that's what you say to all the shewolves. Now, move your ass before you miss your chance."

I saluted once before spinning and running the rest of the way to the stairwell. I flew down the steps, only touching tread on every third one in my haste. By the time I hit the door to the main-floor lobby, I was moving at a full run. Wearing my pack cloak meant I could shift as soon as I reached the front doors. The NALB regional heads didn't want us walking around as wolves indoors, which was fine by me. Wolves were meant to be outdoors, running with nature, not cooped up in some mansion. I raced across the lobby, shoved open the front door, stepped out onto the porch, and—

"Good morning, young man."

—stumbled as I tried to stop my forward momentum. I stood with a glare, only to immediately straighten my shoulders and drop my head in a subtle bow. Blasius Zenne, leader of the entire National Association of the Lycan Brotherhood—the ruling power of wolf shifters across the country—was standing on the porch. I'd seen him from afar at the introduction ceremony, but this was different. The man had more power than any Alpha on the estate, probably more than a few of them combined, yet he stood on the porch like any other shifter.

"Perhaps you couldn't hear me over the noise of the…well, the quiet." The man grinned as I felt my face burn. "Good morning, young man. My name is Blasius Zenne."

I held out my hand, gripping his wrist—as was our custom—when he returned the offer. "I'm Gideon Kelly of the Southern Appalachia pack. It's an honor to meet you, sir."

"Ah, yes," he said with a smile. "Your Alpha has already caused quite the stir around here, hasn't he?"

I pulled my shoulders back and held my chin up. Didn't matter who the guy was, no one spoke ill of my Alpha. "He found his mate, sir. I'm not certain why that would cause any kind of stir."

Blasius stared me down for a long moment. The feeling of such a wolf watching me made me want to jump off the porch and slink into the woods. Instead, I kept my eyes locked on his chin and struggled not to flinch under the weight of his stare.

Finally, he laughed and patted my arm. "You're a good wolf, young man. Loyal to your Alpha. I like to see that."

I snorted a laugh of my own. "Thank you, though it's been a long time since someone called me a young man."

"You're what…almost a hundred years old? Maybe a little over?"

My chest felt hollow as I stared off into the woods. The only thing I couldn't fight was time. "I'm one hundred and eighty-three, to be exact."

"My, you don't seem it. I'm rarely wrong aging a wolf." Blasius moved to stand beside me, facing the woods as well. "Many wolves don't live as long as you have, not without finding their fated mate. You must have a very strong pack structure to fall back on."

I turned to give him an eyebrow raise. "Have you met the O'Sheas? They're kind of a force among themselves."

"I've not had the pleasure yet. I was planning to request a meeting with Killian this afternoon but"—he shrugged and quirked a smile—"interrupting a newly mated wolf might not be in my best interest if I'd like to make a good impression."

"No, probably not. Though Moira's here." When he looked at me with an arched brow, I continued, "Killian's elder sister. She's acting as his official liaison for the pack. I could track her down for you if you'd like."

As soon as the words left my mouth, my stomach clenched. I felt such a need to shift, to search out my mate. Playing host for the leader of the NALB, while quite the honor, would just get in my way.

Blasius watched me for a moment as I struggled to keep from showing how much I didn't want him to say yes. And then he shook his head.

"No, that won't be necessary, Gideon. I can have one of my staff reach her to set up a time to meet. You were in quite the hurry when I interrupted you. Do you mind telling me where you were going?"

I looked out into the woods again, a longing building in

my gut. I was quickly moving beyond need. My urge to be out among the trees was becoming an obsession.

"To shift, to run." I met his eyes for the first time since I'd realized who he was. "To find my mate."

"Ah, then yes. I can see why you'd be in such a rush. A mate, a truly fated partner, is a gift. One never to be taken lightly."

"Are you mated, sir?"

He raised a brow at me. "Such questions aren't usually asked, but yes. I have a mate. We've been together nearly five hundred years already, but unfortunately, we've never found our third."

Triad. The word reverberated through my head. A mating to two others. Rare and secretive, triad matings were something of legend among the packs. Only the strongest of wolves were granted a triad. No normal pack shifter, not even an Alpha, could handle the deep connections the union required. It shouldn't surprise me that the leader of the NALB was in an incomplete triad.

I shrugged, not sure what to say. "Perhaps you'll be lucky and find your third at this Gathering."

"Yes, perhaps." Blasius smiled, though it barely lifted the corners of his mouth. "We started hosting the Gathering as a way to help wolves find their fated mates. I've seen a lot of mating take place at these events, and I've seen a lot of missed connections."

He turned as if heading back inside. "I suggest you run, Gideon Kelly of the Southern Appalachia pack. Give yourself over to your wolf and search out your mate. Even for those of us who live for centuries, time is very precious."

"I will, sir." I moved to step off the porch as he opened the heavy front door. "It was nice meeting you, Blasius."

He gave me a nod. "The pleasure was mine. I'll hunt down your pack liaison later today. I hope to hear good news from her in regards to your mated status."

I stood for a moment staring at the door he'd walked

through, allowing the relief of being out of the presence of such a powerful and dangerous wolf work its way through me. But then my own wolf demanded my attention.

I hurried into the woods, pulling off my cloak along the way. Hanging the blue fabric over a tree limb, I gave myself a moment to enjoy the cool autumn air against my skin.

And then I exploded into my wolf form.

A quick shake of my coat and I was off, running over the rocky ground and through the trees. Staying close to the mansion but not too close. I needed to search, to roam, to find her, to find something. I needed to hunt.

On a pass along the far eastern side of the building, a scent on the air caught my attention. Light and airy, with hints of vanilla and chocolate, it teased my senses and made my heart ache. Every instinct in my body urged me toward it.

My hackles rose as I padded through the tree line, the sense of other wolves nearby putting me on edge. But then I stopped… stared…craved.

On the third-floor balcony stood a woman. Long, flowing red hair danced in the breeze, her pale skin glowing in the morning light as she turned her face into the sun. And her smile. Sweet and true, dark pink lips curling in a way that made my heart bleed for her. A growl bloomed in my chest, deep and powerful as it called for her. I didn't want to hope, was too afraid to be wrong, and yet something about her spoke to me. She could be the one…the other half to my soul…she could be—

Blue eyes bright like a June sky met mine. She'd seen me, heard my growl, and she'd ensnared me in her gaze. My heart raced as everything else fell away, my entire world tilting in her direction.

MATE.

CHAPTER TWO

"THIS MATTER IS NOT UP for debate."

"But, my love, this isn't what she wants."

"It's not what any of us wants, but it's what must be done. For the sake of the pack."

I stepped away from the door and plopped onto the plush carpet. *For the sake of the pack.* Those were words I'd been hearing for as long as I could remember. Being the only Omega female of a small pack was a heavy burden, one I'd been shouldering my entire life. Up until recently, I'd never balked at anything my Alpha asked of me. But this time…this time was a different story. And the reason why my Alpha and his mate were arguing on the other side of the door.

"Not what you wanted to hear?" Micah, my personal bodyguard assigned by the Alpha, gave me an appraising look.

"No. Not in the least." I huffed and fell back to lie on the floor. "This is getting ridiculous. All this security and the extra guard runs. The pack can't survive like this."

Micah gave me a shrug. "We do what we must to keep you

safe, Omega."

"Don't call me that." I turned and glared at him. "You know how much it grates on me when people address me by *what* I am instead of *who* I am."

"True, but I think you need the reminder today." He strolled over, his long and graceful gait eating up the space between us. Tall with lean muscles, he was the epitome of dangerously sexy. His mate, our Alpha's daughter, was one hell of a lucky shewolf.

Micah held out a hand and helped me to my feet before turning me to face the floor-length mirror. "You are the Omega of the Ozanam pack. The bringer of strength and blessings. You're important to us, and therefore, we treat you as something of value. These men collecting Omegas…they won't treat you well if they get ahold of you. They'll destroy the sweet girl we all know. And that would be a huge blow to the entire pack."

I sighed, still unhappy. "I don't want to meet this Beta."

"Our goal is to keep you safe," Micah replied. "If joining with this other pack is a way to do that, so be it. If I have to keep following you all over our pack land to keep you safe, I will. Whatever it takes. Above and beyond the Omega aspect, you are the niece of the Alpha, the daughter of an elder, and the best friend of my wife. The latter of the three being the one I'm most afraid of should something go wrong."

I grinned. "She'd kick your tail."

"She'd cut me off." He grinned as I made a disgusted face. "Go get some sun before the luncheon. I need to call my beautiful, sexy, amazingly-talented-with-her-tongue mate to—"

"Damn, I'll go!" I hurried to the balcony door, pausing just long enough to turn and smile at him. "Thank you. I still think all this fuss is ridiculous, but I understand why it's necessary."

"We just want you safe, Kalie."

I sighed and nodded before stepping outside, relaxing almost instantly in the morning sun. A light breeze blew across the balcony, teasing my hair and skin with its caress. I had an urge to shift and run through the woods below, but I knew it wouldn't be allowed. Ever since the NALB sent word that there was a rogue group of shifters kidnapping Omegas, I hadn't been left alone. No more runs through the trees, no more afternoons at the lake, no more traveling into town to do such simple things as grocery shop and run errands. No, my life now included armed patrols on pack land and a permanent bodyguard.

Damn the so-called power of the Omega in my blood. I just wanted a normal shifter life. But I'd been raised with the mantle of the Omega firmly on my shoulders. Duty. Responsibility. Legacy. All words I'd heard my whole life. I hated them. Hated the way my future had been planned out since I was born. Hated being the only one of my kind in the region. Hated knowing if I didn't find a mate soon, I'd be asked to pair with another wolf to hopefully breed an Omega who would continue in my footsteps. The pressure…it was enormous.

Turning my face up to the sun, I took a deep breath. Aside from the bodyguards and gunmen surrounding me at every moment, the day was lovely. Never mind the fact that in a few hours I'd be meeting the man who might someday join me in my mating season den.

A neighboring pack, one smaller than our own, had requested an alliance. They had a Beta who was strong and fit, a good choice for a partner according to our pack elders. My Alpha felt it would be a good match as it would bring new blood to the pack. A new generation to strengthen us.

Yes, my lineage would continue whether I wanted it to or not. Duty…responsibility…legacy.

Another deep breath to relieve the growing tension in my shoulders, and then I would go back inside. Just a moment to clear my head. I needed a—

I spun, my eyes immediately meeting those of a wolf in the woods. Tall and thick, he stared back at me, his body completely still. Something about him drew me in a way nothing else had.

I wanted to know who he was and why he was looking at me like that. Like I was something he needed. Like I was something he craved.

Unfortunately, before I could move closer to the edge of the balcony, Micah exploded through the doors and grabbed me around my waist. At the same time, two of the armed guards the Alpha had hired rushed out from the building and ran straight for my wolf.

Mine. The word reverberated through my mind. Fitting. Settling into place. He was mine.

My mate.

"No." The word came out as a whisper as terror stole my voice. The guards would kill him if they thought he was a danger to me. I couldn't let that happen. I couldn't watch him die.

"No," I yelled. "Guards, stop. He's no threat."

"Inside, Kalie." Micah pulled me through the door, barely giving me enough time to see as my mate shifted human, his dark, wavy hair and deep eyes the only features I took note of before he was gone.

"Please," I begged, trying to pull out of Micah's grasp. "He's mine. Don't let them hurt him."

Micah pulled me through the bedroom and into the sitting area. My Alpha and his wife jumped to their feet.

"What's happened?" Alpha asked.

"Unknown wolf in the woods." Micah pushed me onto the sofa before slinking to look out the window.

I growled and stood, refusing to be ignored. "He's mine, I'm telling you. Don't you dare let those hired guns hurt him."

Micah gave me a frown as the Alpha female wrapped an arm around my shaking shoulders. "What do you mean, he's yours?"

"He's my mate." I stood tall, my chin raised, as all three of them turned to gape at me. It was my Alpha who finally seemed to work out the meaning of my words.

"Who was he?"

I shook my head, defeat growing heavy in my chest. "I don't know."

CHAPTER THREE

"Stop right there!"

I snarled as two men ran toward me, coming between my mate and me. My hackles rose and I dropped my head as I prepared to fight.

"Shift, wolf."

My snarl turned into barks of warning. The two paused and reached for the guns obviously strapped to their backs. Out of the corner of my eye, I saw a man pulling my mate into the building. Away from me and the danger the men posed. Her eyes were locked on mine, the fear I saw there calling to me. Without thought to the two men in my way, I shifted human. Just in time to see her disappear into the darkness of the mansion.

"Wait, what's your name?" I yelled, but it was too late.

One of the guards chuckled. "Her name is Nunya. Nunya Business. Now go back the way you came before you force us to defend the pride of the Ozanam pack."

I growled, my muscles clenching with the need to kick this idiot's ass. "Pride of...what the hell are you talking about?"

The second man, the one who hadn't spoken yet, lifted a rifle to his shoulder and released the safety. "Either you leave voluntarily or we'll carry you out of here in a body bag. Which would you rather do?"

I put my hands up and took a step back. As much as I wanted to chase after my mate, I knew when to back down. Fists and claws and teeth? I could fight all day. But going up against two men with guns would be suicide. And I'd just found the greatest reason to live the fates had ever given me.

"Fine, I'll go." I backed away slowly, not trusting them to honor their word. I had no idea why my mate was being guarded by such men, but I was determined to find out. Once I figured out how to meet her.

When the two inched back under the balcony, hiding in the shadows there, I shifted to my wolf and ran full bore back the way I'd come. I needed Killian. He might know why she was being guarded and what the pride of a pack meant. I'd never heard Killian or his father before him use that term. Plus, he had a lot more power to get things done than I did. His name would have pull with another Alpha.

Once back where I started, I shifted human, grabbing my blue cloak as I rose to two feet. Refusing to stand still even for a moment, I swung the fabric in an arc around me, darkening the ground as I trod toward the mansion. I fastened the cloak when I hit the stairs and was fully covered when I reached the heavy double doors.

Racing through the entryway, I headed directly for my Alpha's room. I assumed he'd be there with his new mate. And though I hated the thought of interrupting him, I knew he'd understand. I needed access to the woman who was my mate. He'd fight for me to get it.

"Hey, Gideon," Moira said, walking out of the room across from Killian's. "What's got your tail on fire?"

"I need a meeting with the Alpha."

She gave me an appraising look, brows drawn together. "He's down in the pool with his new mate. What is it you need? Perhaps I can help."

I whined, not wanting to disrespect her but also desperate to find Killian and meet the woman on the balcony. Moira had been a friend for a long time and had always been at Killian's side as he moved up the ranks, but she was not an Alpha. Shifters with guns might not respect her title enough to give me a chance with my mate.

"Gideon…what's going on?"

"Mate." My word came out almost on a yell, my human self fighting off a wolf's bark. "I found my mate."

Moira's face transformed with her smile. She'd always been a pretty girl, but when she smiled like that, she was practically breathtaking. "That's wonderful. Killian will be thrilled."

"There's a problem, though." I took a deep breath at her nod. "I don't know her name, I don't know where she's from, and she's under guard for some reason, so I couldn't get near her."

"Under guard?"

"Two men with guns ran me off before I could officially meet her. They called her the 'pride of the Ozanam pack.' I don't know what that means."

Moira tapped a pen against her chin. "Hmmm, well, if she's under guard, she's more than likely an Omega. The NALB offered extra protection to anyone bringing an Omega since the attempted kidnapping involving the Valkoisus pack. I can ask our regional head to direct us to the Ozanam pack; I'm not familiar with that group. If the Alpha won't meet with me, we'll pull Killian away from his new mate and let his cranky ass deal with it."

My shoulders sagged with relief. "Please. Right now, I'll take any help I can get."

"We're the Southern Appalachia pack; no member fights alone." Her lips turned up in a cocky sort of smile as she walked purposefully toward the lobby. "And no one fucks with an O'Shea."

I turned to follow her, excited but nervous. I just wanted to find my mystery mate. I'd do anything, even camp out by the front doors for the next two days for the chance.

We froze when we walked into the lobby area, the sight of a huge, dark wolf running across the room making the two of us stiffen up and drop into a fighting stance. The wolf headed right toward us, sniffing the entire way. He barked once, then shifted human, closing the distance with no regard for his lack of clothing.

"You must come with me," the man growled.

"I don't think so." Moira took a step forward, essentially putting herself between the stranger and me. "As Alpha female, my packmate follows my orders, not yours."

The man looked down at her—at her soft curves and solid O'Shea glare—with something like a smirk. "Is she for real?"

"Pretty much." I crossed my arms over my chest and stepped beside her. "She's been fighting bigger wolves and men than you since before she could walk. I personally wouldn't try to take her without good reason."

The man nodded. "Is your mate good enough of a reason for you?"

My heart paused then raced. "My mate?"

"Yes. Miss Kalie of the Ozanam pack seems to believe you're her mate. I was sent to track you and bring you back to meet her." His face went serious, almost mockingly so. "Unless your Alpha female objects."

"I go with him," Moira said, still looking ready for a fight. "My pack is new to the NALB and is inexperienced when it comes to the dealings between Alphas. I'll act in my Alpha's place to assist him."

The man nodded. "Very well. My name's Micah. If you'll follow me, I'll take you to the Ozanam suites."

We followed the man to the third floor and along the endless corridors until we reached a blockade of three shifters. They moved aside at Micah's nod, though they eyed Moira and me with more than a little distrust.

"What's with all the security?" Moira asked.

Micah glanced over his shoulder. "Kalie's an Omega. We're taking no chances."

Moira gave me a wink as Micah stopped in front of a set of double doors.

"I expect you both to behave." Micah gave us a glare over his shoulder. "And if you even think of hurting Kalie or putting her in danger, I'll string you up by your testicles and leave you for the vultures."

He swung open the doors and strode inside before I could respond. A tall man with broad shoulders turned from where he was speaking with a much smaller woman.

"Ah, Micah. I see you've tracked down our prey."

Micah bowed low. "As you requested, sir."

"Come in, come in." The big man gestured us closer. "My name is Zakris Tobin, and I'm the Alpha of the Ozanam pack. This is my mate, Olivia."

"It's lovely to meet you," Moira said, extending her hand and grasping wrists with Zakris and Olivia as I followed her example. "My name is Moira O'Shea. I'm the soon-to-be-removed Alpha female of Killian O'Shea and acting liaison for the Southern Appalachia pack."

"Soon to be removed?" Olivia asked, looking confused.

Moira smiled. "My brother has found his mate. I'll be handing over the job as soon as she's ready."

"Oh, how wonderful." Olivia clapped and grinned. "This is why I love the Gathering. So many happy couples find their way to each other. I met Zakris at a Gathering many moons ago. Best day of my life."

They smiled sweetly at one another before the Alpha coughed

once and refocused on us. Sans smile.

"I understand you may be the mate of my darling Omega, Kalie."

I gave him a single nod. "Yes, sir. If Kalie is the red-haired woman I saw on a balcony earlier this morning, I believe she's my mate."

"Well, let's just see, then." He turned toward the opposite side of the room. "Kalie…please come meet our guests."

A door swung open, and my mate walked out. Her long, red hair brushed her elbows as she moved, accenting her pale skin. And her curves. Thanks be to the inventor of the cloak, for if I'd been wearing pants, every person in the room would know how hard my sexy mate made me. Long legs, round hips, full breasts…she was an hourglass in human form, completely on display for me in some kind of little dress I rarely saw on pack shewolves. And she was smiling at me.

"Hello," I whispered, finding myself standing in front of her without planning on moving.

"Hello,"—her deep blue eyes locked on mine—"mate."

She grinned as I growled and reached for her. I had to touch her, had to feel how soft I knew she'd be.

"Well, it appears our two young ones have the fates to thank for bringing them together." Zakris laughed and clapped me on the back. "Why don't you two spend a little time together in Kalie's sitting area? Get to know each other while Moira and I talk a little business."

Kalie reached out and tangled her fingers with mine, causing shivers to explode along my spine. Her skin against mine was a drug, an aphrodisiac of some sort. My poor, lonely dick bobbed as I moved, practically begging for her attention.

Hips swaying with every step, Kalie led me back into the room she'd just exited. I pushed the door closed behind me, taking only a brief moment to look over the space. Two couches, a few tables, and glass doors leading to what must have been the balcony where I'd first seen her. One open door led to what was obviously the bedroom. Two more were closed on the far side of the room. Much bigger than my own room at the estate.

We stood in the center of the sitting area, so close we nearly touched. Both of us smiling like loons. Finally, I ran my fingers up her arms to grasp her forearms in a very traditional shifter greeting.

"My name is Gideon Kelly, and I'm from the Southern Appalachia pack in North Carolina."

She bit her lip and edged closer, her breasts making me moan as they pressed against my chest. "I'm Kalie, the Omega from the Ozanam pack in Washington. Though I believe you know most of that already."

"I do." I pulled her even closer, her vanilla and chocolate scent making me crave a taste.

"I'm sure you want to stand here and talk for a few hours." Her grin turned sultry as her hands left my forearms and traced the muscles up and over my biceps. "But I have a luncheon I'm apparently not allowed to miss, which means we don't have a lot of time to get to know each other."

"Luncheon?" I hummed, slipping one leg between hers. "Then I guess we should probably get to this."

I grabbed her by the hips, pulling her along my thigh and flush against me. I'd been hard since I walked in the door, but that move, that pressure, was enough to make my cock throb with need. Fuck, I wanted her. I had to have her.

"Mine." With a growl, I pressed my lips to hers. If I was getting just one shot, it was going to be my best. I put all my wants and needs into the kiss, gripping her tightly to let her know how much I craved her. Hands kneading her ass, thigh pressing against the most intimate part of her, dick nestled snuggly against her stomach, I gave her everything I had.

Chapter Four

I GASPED AS HIS LIPS met mine. Gideon kissed me as if it was our last and not our first. Kissed me as if I was something precious and vital to him. That feeling of being so desperately needed by another made me melt inside.

His hands slid down to my ass, pulling me in tight, pressing the evidence of his desire against me. Our growls grew, each of us being very vocal about our increasing lust. Too vocal. Before the people in the other room could hear us, I broke the kiss and grabbed his hand. When he gave me a curious look, I just smiled and began walking backward.

"Trust me."

He followed willingly, his eyes dark with desire. Fighting off the urge to grab him and press my body against his, I led him to the walk-in closet. I opened the door and dragged him inside, pulling the heavy wooden slab closed behind him without offering an explanation.

"Uh, Kalie?" he asked, his voice questioning but calm. "Are you going to tell me what we're doing in here?"

I grinned in the relative darkness of the cool, quiet room. "I don't think this was always a closet. The walls are virtually soundproof and the door is too solid." I moved closer, pressing my breasts against his chest and looking up at him. "I think it was a hiding space of some kind. And I figured we could use a place to hide so the others wouldn't hear us."

"Hear us doing what exactly?" He slid his hands to my ass again, making me giggle. The man had a thing for the booty. *Noted.*

I rose up onto the balls of my feet and gave his chin a little nip. "Hear us getting to know each other better, of course."

His lips met mine in another fierce kiss, one filled with tension. Damn, the man could kiss. He stroked my tongue like he owned it, moved his lips in a way that had me fighting to keep up. And his hands. The way they kneaded my ass, bunching my skirt, pulling me against his dick with each squeeze. If he kept it up, he was going to have me begging for him in a matter of minutes.

I swayed on my feet as his hands moved lower, his fingers teasing me from behind as I spread my legs for him. Invited him to touch me.

"More," I whispered.

Growl vibrating through his chest, he broke our kiss and dropped to his knees. He lifted the front of my dress, exposing me from the waist down. I almost took a step back, afraid he'd see my soft tummy and be turned off, but he wrapped one arm around my thighs and held me in place. He dropped little kisses along the front of my thighs, my hips, up to my stomach. He nibbled and teased, taking his time to learn every inch he could reach as my hands fisted in his hair.

"Beautiful," he whispered against my flesh as his hands slid around my hips to the front of my thighs.

Craving the feel of his mouth on mine again, I sank to my knees and pulled him into my arms. He kissed me as if we'd been apart for months, not seconds, and I kissed him back with just as much vigor. Needy, desperate for more, I pulled him with me as I lay back onto the carpet. He followed, breathing hard and growling with every exhalation.

"Kalie?"

"We can't claim each other. Not yet." I licked his lips, spreading my legs for him, frustrated that my skirt had fallen back into place and added another layer of interference between us. "But I want. I want."

He nodded, fitting his hips into the cradle of my thighs and grinding his dick against me. "This? You want a little rutting, sweet one? I can do that for you. I can get you off without claiming you."

I hissed a yes, my head thrown back as tingles began racing up and down my spine. He felt so good against me, so strong and solid. And my God, the way the man moved. His entire body undulated on top of me, making the pressure not just focus on my pussy, but all through my body.

"I gotchu, sweet one. I'll take care of you." He lifted himself off me just long enough to pull my skirt up around my waist. "Beautiful. Don't hide from me, Kalie. Let me know you. Teach me you."

I nodded once and pulled my knees up higher, opening myself to him to do with as he pleased. Gideon yanked on the edges of his cloak, our position not allowing me a glimpse of his naked body.

"Tease," I moaned as he once again pressed himself against me. This time was so much better, so much hotter without all that fabric between us. Just the thin cotton of my panties remained in the way.

"A tease would get you all worked up then leave you wanting, sweet one." His lips touched mine, his tongue joining mine for barely a second. "I'm not a tease. I'm going to make sure you come."

I gasped as he thrust hard against me, rolling his body, treating my pussy to pressure and motion unlike I'd ever felt before. My head thumped back against the carpet, my hands clutching at his shoulders as he moved. And his growl. Praise the fates, my mate could growl and kiss and work my body like a pro all at the same time. And I loved it.

The emptiness inside gaped and fluttered, begging to be filled. The pressure increased, the need to come overriding all else.

"Gideon," I cried as the muscles in my legs began to tremble. "Gonna…gonna…"

"Go, Kalie." His speed increased, rutting harder as he groaned. "I won't stop. Never stop. Not until you give it to me, sweet one."

He pressed again and again and again until I bit my bottom lip to stop from screaming and my entire body arched with the power of the orgasm cascading through me. I came and came, shaking through the strongest orgasm of my life. Gideon grunted when I dug my nails into his shoulders, losing his rhythm, his dick pulsing against my stomach as his own orgasm followed mine.

When we were finally spent, lying on the carpet in a heap of sweaty flesh, he gave me a sweet kiss and hummed. "Fuck… that was a bit…"

I giggled and ran my hands up and down the muscles of his arms. "Unexpected?"

He leaned up on his elbow, smiling. "I was going to go with perfect, but unexpected works as well."

He used his cloak to wipe off my stomach, and then pulled my dress back into place, smoothing the fabric over my hips. I gave him another sweet kiss before dropping my head to the floor.

"So I guess we should talk. Maybe know more about each other than just our names."

He shrugged. "We can. Though it doesn't matter."

My heart sank as the possibility of being refused entered my mind. I hadn't thought about it as an option, having felt too drawn to Gideon from the moment I laid eyes on him. But that didn't mean he felt the same.

Fearing the worst, I closed my eyes. "Getting to know me doesn't matter?"

"Nope." He stole another kiss, his voice calm and happy. "You could tell me you're a vegan ecoterrorist with aspirations of someday ridding the world of things like cattle ranches and chicken farms, and I'd still follow you around like a pup."

Relieved, I opened my eyes to meet his, smiling back at him as he grinned. He pulled me on top of him and rolled, ending up underneath me.

"Tell me anything," he whispered, his hands sliding down to grip my ass. "Tell me your worst. I'll still want you, need you, care for you. You're my mate, sweet one. All the rest is just details."

I sighed and frowned. "Well, damn."

His brows drew together. "What?"

"If I didn't have this luncheon to go to, you'd so be getting laid right now."

CHAPTER FIVE

gideon

I wiped my hands on a towel and turned back to the mirror. A wide grin sat upon my face, one I had little control over. My mate. I'd finally found her, and she was everything I could have hoped for. I was truly looking forward to getting to know her better, which meant I needed to leave the bathroom and rejoin her in her suite.

One last check to make sure my cloak fell correctly and my hair wasn't too mussed and I opened the door to join Kalie in the sitting area. She was lounging in a chair, flipping through a magazine. Legs thrown over the arm of the chair, head tilted back, long, red hair curling toward the floor—looking absolutely delicious as a beam of sunlight bathed her in its golden glow.

But when she saw me, when she stood up and smiled, I truly lost my breath. The happy expression on her face, the way her dress skimmed those delicious curves of hers. Amazing. I rushed to her, needing her, growling the whole way.

"You're mine," I whispered as my hands found her hips and I pulled her against me. Her smile turned a bit questioning, but she nodded anyway and gripped my arms. This gorgeous, red-haired angel had fallen into my life, and I would never let her go. I wanted to howl in delight. I wanted to scream from the rooftops that she was mine.

Instead, I leaned down and gave her the sweetest kiss I could, running my tongue along her lips until she opened for me. Stroking, enjoying, subtly claiming the gift the fates had bestowed on me. And then I pulled back.

"Are you sure we can't just stay hidden in your closet for the day?"

Kalie giggled, her head falling to my chest. "I wish. Trust me; I have no interest in this luncheon now that I found you. Not that I ever did."

I pouted as she giggled and rolled her eyes. Our time was up, though. I knew it; I just didn't want to admit it. Finally, after one more taste of her lips, I nodded and released her from my hold. She pulled me toward the door, leading back to the reality awaiting us. Moira, Zakris, and Olivia rose to their feet when we strolled through the door, all three of them grinning.

"I assume by the smiles on your faces that you had a wonderful conversation. Learned a lot about each other," the Alpha said with a grin. Moira brought a hand to her mouth to cover her giggles and Olivia shook with laughter. I threw my arm around Kalie's shoulders, pulling her into my side and smiling at the three of them.

"Sure did. Lots of talking happened. Tons. Pretty sure I know everything about her now."

Alpha Zakris' smile turned downright evil. "What's her last name?"

Well…shit. "Uh…Erickson?"

The three of them laughed, my mate pulling me into her arms and whispering, "Nelson." I shrugged and kissed her forehead, still warmed by the knowledge that she was mine.

When the laughter stopped, the Alpha coughed and nodded

to me. "I appreciate the two of you exercising some restraint. I know how hard it is to deny the need to claim a new mate, but there is no way for me to cancel this luncheon. Kalie will still be introduced to the Beta of the Glaxious pack, but I'll make sure the Alpha is aware that any alliance requiring her commitment to spend mating season with the Beta is no longer an option. I won't break up a fated pair."

I moved in front of Kalie, a growl rumbling through me. "What do you mean? You were going to use her for some kind of—"

"Gideon." Moira's voice was cool and sharp, stopping me immediately. "Zakris was simply going to introduce Kalie to the Beta of this other pack to see if they were agreeable to joining together this mating season."

"It would have had to have been my choice," Kalie said as she came around to face me. I grabbed her, pulling her in, my hands shaking. She gave me a small smile, one that looked more weary than happy. "Gideon, I'm an Omega. A gift to my pack. It's my duty to bear more Omegas so my legacy can continue. Besides"—she ran her hand down the side of my face—"I worried I'd never find my mate, and I've always wanted little ones running underfoot."

I sighed and dropped my forehead to hers as my stomach burned and my wolf spirit clawed at my mind. "I hate this."

"I know," she whispered. "But it's just a lunch. An hour or so at most, and then I'm with you forever."

"I've waited lifetimes for you already; an hour seems so much more torturous now that I've found you."

Her face flushed and a shy smile bloomed. "I'll eat fast."

I pulled her close, tucking her head under my chin and surrounding her with my body as I stared into the eyes of her Alpha. Not afraid of challenging him when it came to my mate.

"I'll sit back and behave for this luncheon, but then your 'duty' is over."

Chapter Six

"Ah, Zakris, old friend." The man welcoming us to the private dining room opened his arms in greeting. Tall and dark, he would have been considered handsome by some had he not carried himself with such an air of…smarminess. "So good to see you. And I see you've brought your lovely Omega."

He reached for my hand, keeping his eyes on mine as he leaned over and brought it to his lips. I forced a smile onto my face even as every bit of my inner wolf growled in protest. I wanted to snap at him for calling me Omega instead of using my name, but I kept my mouth shut. The faster this meeting went, the sooner I could run back to Gideon.

"Kalie, this is Alpha Chilton of the Glaxious pack," Zakris said, his voice harsh.

"Lovely. Seriously lovely, though a little heavy for a pack like ours." He frowned as my eyes darted to his. "We tend to like our women a bit more…lean."

Alpha Zakris gripped my arm as I struggled to hold my tongue. He'd been very clear I was not to speak to the Alpha of this pack. I was here to meet the Beta, eat, and leave. My responsibility to my pack ended there for the day. But this man wasn't making things easy on me.

A wariness suddenly danced up my spine, a feeling of being watched. The sensation made my wolf senses heighten, but I pushed them back. I had a feeling I knew who was hidden outside, looking through the windows.

"Perhaps you could introduce your Beta, Chilton. The two young ones can spend a little time getting to know one another while we discuss business."

"Of course." Chilton snapped his fingers as if calling for some kind of servant. My eyes darted to my Alpha, who shook his head subtly.

The doors at the opposite end of the dining room opened and in strode one of the prettiest men I'd ever seen. Tall and lean, with straight blond hair that practically glittered, I could barely take my eyes off him. Not that I was attracted to him, but he was just so…pretty. There was no other way to describe him.

"Kalie, please meet my Beta, Winslow. I do believe the two of you will find much in common. Winslow, why don't you escort the Omega to your table? I'm sure lunch will be served soon."

"Yes, of course." Winslow extended an arm. I wrapped my fingers around his elbow, almost afraid I'd hurt him if I squeezed too hard. He was practically…breakable. How could such a fine, delicate-looking man be a Beta? The pack second-in-command was usually more of a fighter-type of shifter.

When we reached the table, he pulled out my chair before walking around to his own. "I have to admit, I'm a bit nervous." His smile was shaky as he brought his water glass to his lips.

A flash of gray outside the window caught my attention, and the feeling of being watched increased. It didn't scare me, though. I knew it was my mate skulking through the bushes outside.

Biting back a smile at the thought of Gideon watching me, keeping me safe even when he wasn't allowed in the room with me, I shrugged. "Don't be nervous. I promise not to bite."

Winslow choked, spraying water across his side of the table. "Oh Lord, I'm so sorry. I just…wasn't expecting that."

"Yes, well, I wasn't expecting your Alpha to call me fat. I guess today's been filled with surprises."

Winslow's eyes went wide and his jaw fell open as he stuttered, obviously searching for something to say. I sat back in my chair, hating every single second of this charade. I had no interest in pack politics or making pups with this weakling. I wanted to be wrapped up in the strong arms of my Gideon. I wanted his scent surrounding me and his lips on mine. This farce was a waste of everyone's time.

Another flash of gray in the window. This time closer. I tapped my fingers on the table and bounced my knee, wishing the food would come so I could get this over with. I nearly sighed my thanks when the waiter appeared, until he placed a dish in front of me.

"What the hell is this?"

Winslow glanced over, frowning. "It looks like…salad."

"Well, yes, that I can tell. I guess my question should've been, why am I being served this when you get—" I leaned over my plate to get a good look at his "—prime rib? Is this some kind of joke?"

Winslow coughed and glanced across the room to where our two Alphas seemed to be in an intense and heated debate. "Alpha Chilton portions meals as he sees fit. It's to help keep us in optimum condition."

I rolled my eyes. "That's bullshit."

"That's how you stay alive." His eyes met mine, a layer of strength nearly hiding the fear there. "It's his rules or lights-out. Take your pick."

I swallowed and picked at my salad, suddenly feeling sorry

for the little man across from me. I'd hate to have an Alpha demand that much control, or to live in fear of an Alpha's rage. Zakris and Olivia were, to their core, very kind people. They worked for the good of the pack, not to gain more power over their shifters. There was no fear of death in our pack.

"So," Winslow said after a few awkwardly silent moments. "How many pups would you like to have?"

My eyes darted to his. His face had paled, and he wore a forced smile. He didn't want this alliance any more than I did, of that I was certain. Another streak of gray passing by the window was all it took for me to toss my duty aside and take what I wanted.

"Twelve." I dropped my napkin over the salad plate. "But not with you."

Winslow sat stiff and straight, once again speechless. I shrugged and pointed toward the windows behind him.

"I met my mate this morning, and he's watching me from out there. While you seem like a nice enough guy, you're not what I want."

"Oh, thank fuck." Winslow leaned back in his chair. "No offense, you're downright stunning, but I'm already mated to one-half of my fated triad. We've been trying to convince Chilton to wait for us to find our fated third, but he's convinced we need an Omega in the pack."

"Well, I'm definitely not your girl." I stood and smiled. "This was lovely, but I think it's time for me to go rejoin the man the fates chose for me."

I was turning for the door when he hissed, "Run."

I glanced at him over my shoulder, suddenly seeing the strength of a wolf capable of holding a Beta position. Physically, he may not have been as strong as my Gideon, but the wolf staring back at me definitely held a lot of power.

"Leave your pack and run with your mate. My Alpha doesn't give up easily, and he's got his sights set on an Omega. If you stay so close, he'll come for you. He'll kill anyone in his way to get what he wants."

I glanced across the room where the two Alphas were still arguing, Zakris with his arms crossed over his chest as Chilton gestured wildly.

"What about you?"

He shrugged. "I may be the Beta at Glaxious, but my mate was the sneaky fucker of his pack for years. We won't be heading home when the Gathering is over."

Suddenly feeling a connection to this stranger, I walked to him, leaning over to grip his hand and whisper. "Southern Appalachia pack in North Carolina. That's my mate's pack. If the two of you need sanctuary, I'll gladly speak on your behalf."

"Thank you." He smiled, kind and true and beautiful as he rose from his seat. Gripping my elbows and leaning in to press a soft kiss to my cheek, he said, "I may take you up on that. Now go; your mate is waiting. And probably pissed as hell that I just had my lips against your skin."

I gave him a wink before spinning and sprinting for the door, refusing to stop even as my Alpha called for me. I threw open the doors, allowing them to crash into the walls in my rush to escape. But I couldn't find it in me to care. My mate was nearby, and I was going to find him.

Turning the corner, I saw Gideon striding down the hall toward me. He looked positively menacing as he scowled, the power of his wolf almost a living thing floating around him. He'd come for me, ignoring the rules my Alpha had put in place and rescuing me from the ridiculous luncheon. Damn, that was hot.

When he reached me, his hold wasn't gentle. It was demanding, powerful, and possessive. He gripped me by the arms and yanked me to him, his eyes burning into mine. As the sound of people yelling my name reached my ears, Gideon roared. He pushed me through what looked like a service door, picking me up as he hurried down a small hallway lined with room service trolleys. It was dark in the area where he finally stopped, the shadows pushed back by the light of the single overhead bulb.

Gideon hoisted me onto a stainless steel table set against the wall, breathing hard and growling with every exhalation. My own breathing matched his, my panties growing wetter all the time. Gideon was so hot like this, so strong and in command. I wanted him to take me. Right there in the hallway. To hell with the fact that others could easily interrupt us. I wanted him. Immediately.

Gideon must have felt similarly. Without warning, he grabbed my knees and pulled them around his hips, lining us up. He was so hard, so hot. Fuck, I was practically trembling with how much I wanted him to just…claim. He pushed me down on the tabletop, the cold steel biting into my back as my dress bunched underneath me.

Claws curling around my thighs, eyes on my throat, Gideon leaned forward and ran his nose along my jaw. When he reached my ear, his growl turned to a snarl and he thrust against my pussy.

"Mine."

I groaned and shivered, loving the way that single word made me throb for him. Hell yeah, I was his. Gideon ripped his cloak from his neck and dropped to his knees, licking a trail from my knee to my inner thigh. He grabbed the waistband of my panties and pulled them down my legs, still growling. Still owning.

"Mine."

I nodded, unable to speak as the anticipation built inside of me. Legs shaking, I brought my feet up to his shoulders and let my knees fall to the sides. Gideon growled long and loud as he stood once more, opening me wide and angling my hips. Rocking, the tip of his dick teasing my entrance, he leaned over me and licked my neck.

"Mine."

And then he thrust inside as he bit me.

CHAPTER SEVEN

gideon

FUCK FUCK FUCK FUCK FUCK. The power of her orgasm nearly did me in. Tight, hot, and so very wet, her pussy clenched around me as I buried my teeth in her neck. I probably should have waited, but I couldn't hold back. Watching her with another man had driven my wolf mad. I needed to prove to myself that she was mine—and prove to her that I was a strong enough man and wolf to be worthy of her. I had to claim her.

"Gideon."

I pulled my hips back and worked myself inside once more at her whispered plea, still biting. I would make sure she smelled of me; make sure every wolf in this place knew exactly who she was mated to. And then I'd probably have to beg her forgiveness for biting her in a dirty hallway instead of some place more comfortable and private.

Her fingers raked down my back as she tossed her head, arching into me to ride out her pleasure. I pulled her tighter but couldn't get the right pressure on my dick. Her hot little dress was in the way. I loved it, loved the way it molded to her body, but a cloak would be so much more convenient. I could just yank open the sides to bare her to me. Fuck, I wanted her bare.

My growl intensified as I clung to her neck with my teeth. She whimpered and writhed against me, trying to pull me closer, force me to move faster. But no. I'd had to give up all control to her Alpha, let her go on a date with another man. I needed to run this show.

Finally, with a lick and a deep growl, I released her neck, moving as if to press my lips to hers. I held myself just over top of her, lips brushing, refusing to give her the sweetness of my kiss just yet. I had to pull my wolf back if I didn't want to scare her, but fuck, it was hard. Watching her with that other man had been brutal, and when he'd touched her—dared to kiss her cheek—I'd lost it. I'd rushed inside, preparing for a fight. I had no idea Kalie would be running away from him and toward me at the same time.

"Mine." The word came out long and hisslike as my growl gave it an undertone. My wolf was still in fight mode, ready to challenge anyone who tried to take my mate away. I feared Kalie would be put off by such an aggressive display, but she seemed to like it.

"Yes," she yelled. "Yes, yours. Please. Please take me. Claim me."

Head back, lips swollen and red, chest heaving, she was lust personified. Snarling as I began to thrust in earnest, I ripped the offending dress open. She gasped and moaned as her breasts met the cold air of the hall, but my eyes were locked on her chest. Gorgeous, full, with peach nipples made for sucking, she had the most perfect breasts I'd ever seen. I wanted to spend hours worshiping them with my mouth and fingers. Wanted to hold them together and slide my dick inside. Fuck, I had to taste them.

I lifted one of Kalie's legs until her knee rested across my shoulder. Leaning over her, I took her hardened nipple into my mouth. Sucking, licking, teasing, I continued working my dick deep as I played with her breast. Teased it. Her hands gripped my hair, pulling and holding me in place against her flesh. Not that she needed to. I'd suckle her gorgeous nipples all day.

But the position wouldn't allow me to go deep enough. I lifted her legs, angled her hips, and yet my wolf couldn't be satisfied. Growling, pumping my hips, I tried and tried to get deeper, work her harder, but something restricted me.

As if sensing my dilemma, Kalie pulled my head to hers and bit my bottom lip. *Fuck.*

"Do it. Claim me, Gideon. I can feel your frustration." Her eyes met mine, filled with need and trust and desire. "Fuck me how you need to, my wolf."

I roared as my wolf spirit rose within. Taking a step back, I slid out of her. Gripped her hips, flipped her to her stomach. She gasped, probably from the metal meeting the heated flesh of her breasts. But my wolf didn't care because her beautiful pink pussy was completely on display in this position. Needing more skin, more of her, I ripped her dress again, opening a line from neck to hem. Giving me the perfect view of her back and spine.

Completely desperate to taste more of my mate, I dropped to my knees, pressing my mouth to her pussy and lapping from her opening to the hood of her clit. Once, twice, three times, savoring the flavor of her on my tongue, growing harder with every whimper and moan she released. Pulling her by her knees, I edged her farther down, putting her in the perfect position. Ass over the edge, hands gripping the sides, fabric of her destroyed dress hanging from her arms, she trembled and growled while I ate her. My dick throbbed, practically screaming to be back inside her, but I needed another minute. Just a few more laps of her sweetness.

But when she wrapped her ankles around the legs of the trolley, opening herself even wider for me, I couldn't resist any longer. I jumped to my feet, crowding against her ass, nudging her opening with my weeping dick.

I growled long and low, loving the way the sound made goose bumps rise on her flesh. "Ready for me, mate?"

She groaned a yes, her fists clenching the edges of the table. I slid the head of my dick over her clit, giving her a little tease, a little extra stimulation. On the third pass, I stopped the teasing and plunged inside her. She gasped, her back arching, but I didn't let her pull away. I fucked her hard and deep, my wolf finally happy with how I had her pinned beneath me. Laid out. Head down, ass up, completely open to me. Beautiful.

Gripping her hips, I thrust into her over and over, taking her the way I needed to. And if her groans and growls and muttered curse words were any indication, she liked what I was doing.

Wanting her to come again, I laid my chest along her back. I slid one arm up and under hers, ending with my forearm supporting her head. I edged my other arm around her hip, working my hand forward until my fingertips reached where we were joined. Running the pads through her wetness, loving the feeling of my dick sliding in and out, I twisted my hand to press my finger against her clit.

Underneath me, Kalie yelped, her body trembling. Close, she was so close. I worked that stubborn clit, rubbing circles and adding pressure with each pass. Building her up. Holding back my own orgasm as I waited for her.

"Yes. Yes. Yes." Kalie growled and punched the table near her head, her entire body clenching in anticipation of her orgasm. I continued filling her, teasing that little clit of hers, giving her body what she needed as I claimed her. Because that's exactly what this was—a claiming. Hot, sexy, and totally in my control, Kalie was giving in to my needs while I strived to fulfill hers.

Her pussy fluttered around my dick and she yelled my name, claws appearing on her fingertips as she lost a bit of control over her wolf. Fuck, that was hot. Between the visual reminder of both sides of her spirit and the way her pussy milked my dick, I couldn't hold back. I thrust messily, anticipating the fall over the final edge of my orgasm.

But then Kalie clamped down on my forearm, biting me. Claiming *me*. I roared my satisfaction, coming stronger and harder than ever before. I felt every wave, every muscle clench, every stream filling her. Felt the satisfaction of her wolf. Relished the relief of mine. The orgasm completely took me over. My entire reality turned hazy, the only thing I was certain of being Kalie beneath me. With her teeth buried in my arm.

CHAPTER EIGHT

As everything came back into focus, I snuggled on top of my mate. Our sweat-soaked skin stuck together, and our breathing synched. Kalie was lapping at my arm, making a sound too much like a purr to be a true growl. But whatever it was, I liked it.

"Happy, mate?" I asked just before I gave her shoulder blade a gentle nip.

Kalie hummed. "Very much so."

I cuddled her close, clinging to her even as my hands traveled over every inch of skin I could reach. She needed to be spoiled and deserved to know how precious she was to me. I would have happily stayed right there in that dark and empty hallway proving my ability to care for her, but after a few moments, she sighed and lifted up on her arms.

"You know what would make me even happier?"

"What's that?" I licked a line up her spine, from the top of her ass to the nape of her neck, ending with a tiny nibble.

"If I didn't have come dripping down my thighs."

I chuckled and slid off her, not wanting her to be uncomfortable. She moved as if to get up, but I held her down against the table, letting my eyes take their fill. Red hair mussed, torn dress dangling from her elbows and brushing the floor, skin flushed, bent over the edge of the table, pussy swollen, pink, and covered with evidence of the two of us.

"Perfect," I growled as I appreciated the view.

She looked at me over her shoulder, a smirk on her lips. "You're just a bit dirty, aren't you?"

I ran my thumbs along the sides of her pussy, pulling her open, holding her gaze. Sliding one thumb inside, I pumped in and out until the digit was good and wet. I let her go, bringing the thumb to my mouth and licking it clean. Watching her the entire time. Growling as her eyes darkened and her breathing picked up. And then I grinned.

"Do you mind?"

She huffed a laugh. "Hell no."

"Good, because I'm not done with you yet." I gripped her hips and pulled her off the table. She spun and wrapped her arms around me, her skin cold where it'd been pressed against the metal.

"How about we head back to my room so I can clean up?" She bit her lip and took a step back, looking me over from head to toe. "I think it's my turn to throw you down and have my way with you."

I laughed, stalking her as she backed away from me. "You think so, huh?"

She nodded, her smirk turning to a grin. "Yup. I have a bit of a fantasy I think you might enjoy."

I growled and closed the distance between us, yanking her into my arms. "Fantasy?"

She nodded slowly, watching me. Enticing me. Making me happy with nothing more than a look.

"I'd do anything for you." My promise came out as a whisper, but the truth behind it didn't need volume. I tangled my fingers with Kalie's and brought our joined hands up. Keeping my eyes on hers, I nuzzled her palm, loving the feel of her flesh against mine, of her scent all around me.

"My mate," Kalie whispered. She rocked onto the balls of her feet to give me a kiss. "C'mon, handsome. Let's go find a private den to hole up in for the day."

I nodded my acceptance, excited with the possibility of just being alone with her. We could truly get to know one another in more than just the physical sense. Not that I'd turn down a little more how-you-doin' physicality. Just watching her ass sway as she walked away had me hard and desperate for her again. Her very bare ass.

"Hang on." I ran over and picked up my cloak from where it lay against the wall. Shaking it out, I hurried back to her so I could drape the fabric around her shoulders. "You can't walk around the hotel like that."

She smiled and pulled the torn fabric of her dress from her arms before fastening the cloak. "Yeah, I guess you did kill my poor dress."

I shrugged. "I hated it."

"Me too. I'd much rather be wearing your cloak. But what about you?"

"I'm sure I'm not the first man who's had to walk back to his room naked at a Gathering."

She laughed and led me down the hall. Luckily for me, the estate was relatively quiet. We only passed a few people on our way to her suite, all of them grinning. Beyond the fact that I was missing my clothes and the cloak Kalie wore was obviously too large for her, they had to smell the way our scents mingled. There was no doubting what we'd done or who we were to each other. And that made my wolf proud.

CHAPTER NINE

I STUMBLED INTO THE MAIN room of my Alpha's suite, laughing as Gideon tickled my side. The tension in the room was a physical thing, though, making my smile fall. Moira and a man I didn't know were sitting with Zakris and Olivia, all talking quietly. None of them looked particularly thrilled.

"What's up?" I asked as Gideon pulled me into his side. He must have felt the same tension I did, his wolf reacting with a quiet growl and a wariness evidenced by his stiff stance. Micah slipped in the door behind us, tossing Gideon a black cloak as he passed us. I felt my cheeks burn as I realized he must have been nearby when we...when Gideon and I...in the hallway. *Oh hell.*

Alpha Zakris stood, his face grim even as he forced a smile. "The mated couple returns. Congratulations, my dear Kalie. I'm so happy for you."

I nodded my thanks, unable to move toward him as Gideon clung to my side. "Thank you, Alpha."

"If you're so happy, why do you and Moira look like

someone's died?" Gideon asked. "And why is Cahill here?"

Moira stood, her eyes darting to my mate. "We've been talking about your future, and we have a request. With the threat of the Omega kidnapper and the alliance with the Ozanam's neighboring pack no longer an option, Zakris feels Kalie might be safer if she came with us to North Carolina."

She turned to me, her face serious. "I know how much you'll miss your pack, but your safety is our priority. Our position in the mountains offers us a natural defense, plus our wolves are strong. You can see how large Gideon is, and he's not even one of our guards. Cahill here"—she gestured to the muscular blond man standing beside her—"is the head of pack security and would be in charge of making sure you and Gideon remained safe. We're a strong pack, a large one, and would be a better team to have on your side should anyone attempt to get close to you."

Gideon looked down at me, a question in his eyes. Where we would live was my decision, and I definitely wanted to go home. But after the warning from Winslow, and knowing how much of a toll guarding me would take on my pack, I had to admit moving to North Carolina was the smarter option. Leaving the Ozanam pack was a way to fulfill my responsibility to them, to care for them. A way to do my duty as Omega.

I took a deep breath and kept my eyes on Gideon, needing a little of his strength. "I absolve my loyalty to the Ozanam pack and request acceptance from the Southern Appalachia pack."

Gideon grinned, looking slightly proud as he spoke in a clear voice. "I present Omega Kalie Nelson as my mate, and I ask for her to be accepted into the Southern Appalachia pack officially."

"And so it's done." Moira nodded at Zakris before turning to give me a broad smile. "Welcome, Kalie. I'm honored to have you as an addition to our family."

"Thank you," I whispered as Gideon pulled me tighter to his side. I glanced at my Alpha and his wife. They both smiled at me, but there was a sadness in their eyes. A loss. I felt it as well. I'd miss my friends from Ozanam, but I was excited for a future with Gideon.

"Now, if you'll all excuse us," Moira said as she headed for the door. "I need to find Killian and give him the good news. You two should go straighten up. Cahill and Micah will be discussing strategy to coordinate the move to North Carolina."

She stopped, sending a hard look to Gideon. "Do not leave this suite without one of the guards with you. Your mate is someone precious, someone to be protected at all times."

Gideon growled and nodded. "Yes, ma'am."

As everyone around us moved on to other things, Gideon leaned down to kiss my forehead. "C'mon, mate. Let's get you cleaned up."

After a quick shower—alone, sadly—I found Gideon standing in my closet. The space still smelled like us, like sex and desire. It made me wet just walking into the room, and I wondered if the scent had the same effect on my mate. I walked up behind him, curling my body into his and running my hands along his thighs. Teasing his definitely hard dick through the rough fabric of the cloak he wore.

"What are you up to, mate?" I asked.

"Just thinking." He groaned as I wrapped my hand around his length, finding him hard and ready.

"Thinking about what?" I stroked him, my other hand pulling aside the fabric of his cloak so I could feel his skin against mine.

Thrusting into my palm, he growled, "About fucking you."

He swung me around to the front of him, the muscles in his arms bulging with the effort. His strength turned me on, made me crazy with my desire to have him holding me, supporting me, buried deep inside me. I'd had a fantasy about this very closet since I first saw it, about clinging to the closet rod over my head and having someone pound into me. Someone with the strength to hold me up in case I let go of the bar. That someone was going to be my Gideon.

I gave him a smile as I took a step back, stretching onto my toes to grab the closet rod above my head.

"I kind of can't get a certain fantasy out of my head."

"The fantasy of me fucking you?" He stalked to me, grabbed my hips, and lifted me so my legs wrapped around him. Lining us up. The towel I'd wrapped around me fell to the floor, leaving me bare for him.

I pulled on the closet rod, keeping my arms spread wide. "Yes…mostly."

He leaned forward, biting my lip and growling. "In your closet? You want me to hold you up and fuck you right here, don't you?"

"Yes," I hissed as he teased my pussy, nudging the tip of his dick against me. I dropped my head back as he pulled me closer, working his hips against me and sliding inside. "Please."

"As you wish." He thrust hard, filling me in a single stroke as his hands clutched my hips. His grip was brutal and damn near painful, but I loved it.

It didn't take long for me to lose my grasp, too focused on the way the base of his dick pressed against my clit with every thrust to bother holding on. When I released the bar and fell to his shoulders, he pushed me against the wall. And then he let himself go. Pumping his hips, squeezing my ass, biting my neck and shoulder. I clung to him, loving the way he felt inside me. The way he filled me. Fuck, he was practically breaking me in two, and I couldn't get enough.

He adjusted his grip, angling me a new way, sliding even deeper. I gasped and shivered, the feeling of my impending orgasm quickly taking over.

"Oh, gonna…Gideon, I'm gonna—"

"Let go, sweet one," he growled. "I gotchu, just let go."

I nodded into his neck while the pressure building low in

my abdomen expanded. As my orgasm crested and every muscle in my body prepared to lock down, I bit down on Gideon's shoulder. Reclaiming him. Fuck, the taste of him on my tongue threw me headlong into another intense orgasm, my entire body shaking with the release. Gideon thrust and jerked, finally groaning his completion as his teeth closed around the flesh of my shoulder.

After several minutes of shallow thrusts, claiming bites, and wandering hands, Gideon released my flesh from his jaws and whispered, "That's two."

I hummed and licked a path up his neck. "We're going to be covered in scars if we don't stop."

"Never," he said, tightening his hold on my ass. "I'll never stop wanting to claim you, Kalie."

"Thank the fates for that."

"Totally." He kissed my neck and nibbled on my earlobe before murmuring, "I have a large cabin on an overlook that gives me one of the nicest views of the mountains on pack property. You'll love it."

I nodded and clung to him, my anchor in the sea of uncertainty swirling around me. "I'm sure I will."

"I also have closets. Lots and lots of closets."

Day Three

blasius, dante & moira

CHAPTER ONE

moira

SEQUINED DRESSES AND HIGH HEELS had become my enemies. I rolled and shoved, packing away the beautiful garments I'd brought with me with a lot less care than I normally would have. It wasn't as if I was going to get a chance to wear them.

Tonight was the last night of the Gathering, the yearly social event to politick, party, and proliferate. Or at least to have the opportunity to meet other wolf shifters in the hope of finding a fated mate. The last night of the event was supposed to be the wildest and most raucous party of the weekend. But was I going? No. I was spending my evening in baggy shorts and a T-shirt, packing my bags to go back to North Carolina, and prepping for a meeting with the National Association of the Lycan Brotherhood leadership in the morning. That last one was a job Killian, my brother and the Alpha of our pack, should have been doing. Unfortunately, he'd abandoned all of his responsibilities the moment he met his fated mate.

The bastard.

I sighed as I grabbed my favorite dress. Turquoise silk, fitted through the hips, backless, with a single jeweled strap as an accent. It was beautiful and elegant. And not something I'd be wearing. I hung it on the back of the door and slumped to the floor. I hated that I felt this way, that jealousy and loneliness were stealing what should have been a happy time for our pack. Killian had been alone just as long as I had, and he had the impossible job of leading our rabble-rousing pack without killing anyone. He deserved to find his fated mate.

In fact, after two decades without a single fated union, six of our packmates had found their mates at the Gathering. The fates had smiled down on them. I didn't begrudge their luck; I just wished I'd been smiled on as well.

I heard my brother coming long before he reached my door, his husky laugh and the soft giggle of his mate traveling down the hall. Wallowing would have to wait, apparently. I had the door open and a smile plastered on my face before he could knock.

"Killian, Lyra. Come in. Why aren't you at the party?"

Killian, dressed in a tailored black suit, looked more handsome than ever, almost debonair. Except for the tie he simply refused to leave alone at his throat. I straightened the silk as he grimaced at Lyra, his new mate.

"Told you. There was no way she was going to leave that alone."

Lyra grinned, her dark hair spilling over the top of her hot pink dress in perfect waves. "Maybe if you could stop fidgeting with it, we wouldn't have to keep tightening it." Lyra winked at me as I stepped back, the tie perfectly knotted once more.

"Your new mate is wise."

Killian growled. "I hate these fucking things."

"I know," Lyra and I said in unison.

"The two of you cannot band together," Killian said, pointing his finger from Lyra to me and scowling. "I'm completely fucked if you do."

"At least he recognizes it," Lyra said with a shrug.

"Oh yeah. He may act like a child, but he's not dumb."

"You two scare me." But Killian's smile betrayed his real feelings. He looked truly happy, something I hadn't seen him be in a number of years. A pang of hurt exploded in my heart even as my eyes filled with joyous tears. I loved seeing him like this; I honestly did. But damn it, I wanted it for myself as well.

"Why aren't you dressed?" Lyra asked.

I waved her off, fighting to remain casual. "Ah, big parties aren't my thing. Besides, I have packing to do and the meeting with the president of the NALB to prepare for. There's no time for drunken craziness."

Killian frowned. "I'm really sorry I wasn't around today, sis."

"It's no bother," I lied. "I handled the mating negotiations for you. The only one we need to be concerned about is Gideon—his mate is an Omega and will need additional security."

"You should get Cahill—"

"Already done."

He leaned forward, giving me a quick kiss on the forehead. "You are the absolute best."

"I've heard that from you before."

"And you'll hear it again." He wrapped an arm around Lyra's waist and pulled her into his side. "So tomorrow we meet with the biggest bigwig here and then we head home."

I shrugged. "Pretty much."

"Got it." He glanced down at his mate. "You ready to go kick up your heels?"

"Damn straight, though can you not toss me over your shoulder this time? I don't need to flash the crowd again."

"Are you wearing those strappy things under there?" Killian asked, a wolfish grin on his face as he tried to slip his fingers under Lyra's skirt. His mate, thankfully, was too fast for him and smacked his wandering hand.

"You'll only get to find out after the party. I want to dance and have fun."

"We have f—"

"Outside-the-bedroom fun." She sighed as Killian's eyebrows rose. "Fun that can be had in front of other people, you perv."

"Well, technically—"

"Okay," I interrupted, not needing to hear whatever my brother had to say. "You two have a good time. I'll see you in the morning."

They waved goodbye as they walked out, Killian grabbing Lyra just outside the door and throwing her over his shoulder. He sang an old drinking song my dad liked as he ran down the hall, Lyra smacking him the whole way. The guy was acting a fool, but he was also filled with a bliss to be envious of. I couldn't help but be thankful and delighted on his behalf.

I went back to my packing and moping, finally moving on to meeting prep once my bags were filled. I didn't realize how long I'd been reading over NALB regulations until I heard Gideon and his new mate, Kalie, coming down the hallway. When their door slammed, I went back to my reading, but soon enough, the sounds of their impassioned after-party activities drifted through the walls. Wonderful. So not only was I not at the party, I was going to be subjected to listening to the two of them getting it on all night long.

It wasn't as if the sounds of men and women having sex bothered me. But at home, at least I had a couple of male packmates to work out my frustrations with. We had spent many an afternoon in the woods, being completely free with each other in twos and threes. Unfortunately, none of them was my mate. So, while I'd had plenty of sex, I'd never felt the love and peace that I saw in Killian since he met Lyra.

And that Gideon and Kalie were channeling as they banged and thumped and growled.

Closing my NALB handbook, I spied my blue dress still hanging from the closet door. Screw it. Between the noise and the overall frustration twisting me up inside, I wasn't going to get any work done. I could go down to the party for a little while, meet people, mingle. Besides, it'd been too long since I'd been the one being banged and thumped and growled at.

I grabbed the dress off the door and hurried into the bathroom. A few drinks, a dance or two, and perhaps even a night spent in the company of a handsome wolf. If I couldn't find my forever, perhaps I'd be lucky enough to find my for-the-moment.

CHAPTER TWO

"You seem tense."

Blaze kept his eyes on the crowd below as he sighed. "I'm more tired than tense."

I ran my hand across his hip and leaned into his shoulder. "Too bad. Tense I can help with. Tired isn't exactly in my wheelhouse."

He smiled, turning just enough to meet my gaze. "You're much better at making me tired than keeping me from being tired."

"Are you complaining?"

"Not for a second." He leaned forward, pressing his lips to mine in a soft kiss before returning to stare out over the crowd of shifters. It was the last night of the Gathering, and the final party below was in full swing. "Whatever happened to this being an elegant affair?"

"Our nature happened. Wolves like sex, so the evening became about finding it." I watched as men and women flirted, kissed, and even tried to be subtle as they moved from public displays of affection to public indecency right there in the ballroom. Not that anyone would be complaining. Most of the people with their pants unzipped and their dresses hiked up probably enjoyed all the eyes on them.

The final party was always like this—one big celebration of our animal instincts but in our human forms. Lust and alcohol, sexy dresses and horny men led to what was considered by many to be the highlight of the Gathering every year. Blaze and I used to partake, oftentimes bringing a willing wolf, male or female, into our bed for the night. Unfortunately, as time went on and he climbed the ranks of the NALB leadership, Blaze had become more and more withdrawn at the event. More stressed. Less present. So instead of dancing and talking with our fellow shifters, we stood on a balcony overlooking the festivities. Hiding behind the lights.

I knew he was frustrated. We'd been mated for five centuries, but we'd never been a complete set. From the moment we met, we knew we were missing our third mate. It was a feeling of incompleteness, of loneliness that no amount of time together could negate.

For the past seventy-eight years, we'd hosted the Gathering as a way for fated mates to meet. And every year, the fates dashed our hopes as couples found one another but left us without. The emptiness between us had grown, the feelings of not being enough weighing us down, especially since Blaze had taken on the role of president of the National Association of the Lycan Brotherhood. A job that took him away from me more often than I cared for.

"You've given up hope," I said, not looking at him.

He sighed. "I've stopped searching."

"But she's out there somewhere."

"Yes, as we've said for centuries. She's out there; we just have to find her. Well, I'm tired of looking and being disappointed."

"What if she's looking for us?"

He spun, his body looming over mine as he advanced on me. "How much more visible can I be, Dante? I've plotted, fought, and clawed my way to the very top, to the most powerful seat in the shifter community. I've traveled to almost every pack, met thousands upon thousands of shifters from across the world. Wolves, bears, tigers, lions, fucking llamas…and still nothing."

He balled his hands into fists, his chest heaving. I reached for him, running my hand down the side of his beautiful face.

"You're really upset."

"I'm…on edge. My inner beast is scratching to get out." He dropped his head, blond waves hiding his face from me. "I can't settle myself down."

I pulled him closer, pressing him against me, lifting his chin with my fingers. "Maybe you need a good run."

Blaze chuffed and peered at me, his eyes nearly glowing with the power of his wolf spirit. The look he gave me was carnal, one full of need and desire. That look spoke to my wild side, made my claiming bite burn and my cock grow hard in an instant.

"I think I need more than just a run."

Blaze shoved me against the wall. I clutched at his shoulders and searched out his lips, opening my own to his probing tongue. Hips pressed tight, we moved in a well-practiced rhythm, rubbing our cocks together through the ridiculous dress pants we wore. I wanted him naked, wanted to strip him of the mask he wore when in front of the people he led, so I could see the real him. The man in the suit was not my Blaze. He was Blasius Zenne, president of the National Association of the Lycan Brotherhood, the shifter with the biggest target on his back in our world. And there were times when I hated him. Hated that this facade was slowly killing my charming mate. *My* Blaze. The man who laughed and joked and gave the best fucking blow jobs known to man or beast.

Knowing I needed to take what I could get while Blaze was offering it, I ran my hands over his ass, pulling him in tighter, practically wrapping myself around him in my effort to get closer. Fuck, he felt good. All hard muscle and hard cock, with soft lips that knew exactly how to kiss me. How to move with mine. How to make me whimper into his mouth. Desperate for more, wanting to feel his skin on mine, I reached between us to unzip his pants.

And then we both froze.

"What was that?" I asked, my voice quiet as I panted through my words.

Blaze turned, pushing me behind him as he moved from the shadows to look over the crowd. I rolled my eyes at his antics. I was almost as big as he was and much stronger than most of the Alphas at this event. I didn't need him to fight my battles for me. But as the higher-ranking wolf in our pairing, his instinct was to put himself between danger and me. The dumbass.

Looking over the crowd, I watched as a woman in bright blue glided across the floor. Something about her drew me in, refused to let me look away. Elegant and stunning, she practically sucked the air right out of the room. True, in her floor-length gown, she stood out against the crowd of miniskirted women, but it wasn't her dress that called to me. It was simply…her.

"Could it be?" I asked, breathless.

"I…" Blaze faltered, swallowing hard as he watched her. Hunted her. His eyes glowing more golden with every second. "I'm almost afraid to hope."

She approached another couple, smiling widely. The man was huge, towering over the woman at his side, and quite obviously an Alpha.

"Killian O'Shea." Blaze leaned forward, his gaze intense. "She's talking to Killian O'Shea from the Southern Appalachia pack."

"We have yet to meet the new Alpha," I said, hope filling me with purpose. "We have a meeting scheduled with him in the morning, but perhaps we should go down there. Introduce ourselves to our newest pack leader at a more social event."

Blaze nodded, still staring. "She may not be—"

"But if she is—"

He looked at me, a fear I hadn't seen in many years upon his face. "Dante."

"Let us see, my love." I palmed the side of his face and pressed my lips to his in a soft kiss. "Let us hope."

Chapter Three

moira

"I'm so glad you decided to get off your ass and come down here." Killian grinned at me, his eyes just a bit unfocused. "What'd you say to me last night? Something about dragging my cranky ass across the country if I didn't find my mate? Maybe I should do the same for you."

He leaned forward and wrapped an arm around my shoulders, pulling me in for a kiss to the top of my head. He always had been such a loveable drunk.

"Smartass." I pulled out of his hold. "You'd better just be happy you did find your mate. Otherwise, I was throwing you in the back of a van."

He smiled down at Lyra, happiness radiating off the two of them. "Trust me; I'm the luckiest man in the world right now, and I know it."

Lyra grinned and rose up on the balls of her feet to kiss him, but her smile faltered as she glanced over his shoulder. Curling into his side, she practically cowered. I spun, ready to defend her from whatever had her so afraid, only to come face-to-face with her former Alpha. A man my brother had appropriately nicknamed Oily Fucker.

"Miss Moira, it's a pleasure to see you here this evening." He reached for my hand, leaning over it and bringing his dry lips to the back. I had to fight the urge to roll my eyes at his act. I knew exactly what kind of a misogynistic jackass he was.

"Alpha—" I froze, desperately searching my memory for his real name, which was on the tip of my "—Kosrath. How nice to see you again. Are you enjoying the party?"

As Killian began to growl, I stepped toward the man, directing him back the way he came. The last thing we needed was for my brother to go all caveman on this pissant jerk. True, the guy deserved it for trying to get between Killian and his mate, but that didn't mean I'd let my brother embarrass our pack. This was our first Gathering; we needed to make a good impression on the NALB leadership. And considering Killian had literally thrown Lyra over his shoulder at the black-tie dinner the first night and carted her out of the ballroom like a Neanderthal, it was probably going to be an uphill battle.

Mr. Short, Dark, and Not-at-All Handsome waved his hand, completely dismissing the crowd. "These events are so tedious. I much prefer a more intimate venue for my social engagements."

"Yes, I'm sure." I scowled over my shoulder at my brother and gave Lyra a head nod to let her know I'd take care of things as I led Alpha Kosrath away from the couple. Once again, I was forced to take on a shit job to save my pack from my brother's assholeish behavior. It was a good thing I was such a talented actress, otherwise this oily fucker would know exactly how little I wanted to be anywhere near him. Killian so owed me for this one.

I hummed and nodded as Kosrath recounted all the very important—in his own mind—meetings he'd had that day, not that I was really listening. For one thing, the man was a pompous jerk. For another, an itch had formed on the back of my neck, a sudden knowledge of being watched that made me anxious. Not bad anxious, though. I didn't feel in danger, just… observed.

"So I told him if he wanted to mingle with the plebeians, he should take that nasty Draught those Feral Breed beasts brew and head for the hills. Leave us more civilized packs to ourselves."

"Yes, yes, I can see that." I glanced around the room, searching out something to explain the way my heart was suddenly racing, and ignoring the growing tension in my gut. The one that spoke of need, desire…arousal.

There.

Two men, standing in the shadows at the far side of the dance floor. Staring right at me.

"It's such a pleasant surprise that you haven't been corrupted by your ignorant brother."

"Yes, of course—" I spun and glared as his words registered. "Excuse me?"

Kosrath smiled, looking at me with a patronizing expression on his face as if I hadn't comprehended what he'd said. "I was afraid after his deplorable manners that you'd be just as backwoods as him, but it appears my fears were unfounded. You're positively lovely, Miss Moira."

"I don't—" My eyes were drawn back across the floor. The men had moved, circling around, coming closer as they continued watching me. I couldn't concentrate on Kosrath and his arrogant opinions, couldn't think past the need to investigate the two men draped in shadows. Who were they, what made them stare at me like that, and why the hell was my wolf spirit suddenly clawing at my consciousness to break free?

As the men moved closer, they stepped into a stream of light shining down from the ceiling. The harshness of the beam threw their faces into shadow, but I managed to get a better look at them. One light-haired, one dark, both muscular and graceful.

I could feel their eyes on me, the way they stared. The way they made me want to never look away.

"I love this dress. I can't wait to see it on my floor."

I opened my mouth to ask the oily fucker what the hell he thought he was saying, but I was too late. His hands gripped my arms and he pulled me against him, his lips crashing down on mine. Eyes wide, mouth open and vulnerable to the assault of his overly wet tongue, I did the first thing I could think of. I brought my knee up and kicked him in the balls.

He grunted, buckling over as he tried to hang on to me. I didn't even pause. The men who'd been watching me were leaving, rushing away toward a dark corridor off the main room. I hurried after them, needing to see their faces. Desperate to know who they were and which one I was so attracted to.

And tamping down the hope that I'd just seen my mate for the very first time.

CHAPTER FOUR

dante

I GRAPPLED WITH BLAZE, SHOVING him off the dance floor and toward the service corridors. Not that I blamed him for trying to rush the asshole who'd just kissed an obviously reluctant woman in our midst. But years of being by his side had taught me many things, one of which was that half the Alphas in the room would happily cut off his head for a chance at the seat of power he held. And as strong as he was, Blaze had one huge weakness. Well, two now.

His mates.

"I'm going to kill him." Blaze growled through his words, his body taut, and his face as filled with rage as I'd ever seen.

"Yes, I know." I kept him moving down the corridor, deeper into the labyrinth of halls leading to God only knew where.

"We can't leave her alone out there." He tried to push past me, but I braced my feet and held my ground.

"If the way the man crumpled in pain is any indication, I'm pretty sure she's just fine." I replayed how our mate had introduced Alpha Kosrath to her knee, a loop that made me want to commend her. The man was a jackass. "Besides, her brother was already storming his way across the room."

Blaze paused, his eyebrows scrunched together. "Her brother?"

"Yes, now go." I shoved him farther down the hall, checking behind me to make sure no one could see us. "Killian O'Shea, Alpha of the Southern Appalachia pack is her brother. They look too much alike not to be related. Which means she's the lauded Moira O'Shea."

"She's Moira O'Shea? The one I've been trying to get a meeting with all damned day?" he asked, his voice rising with each word.

"Yes," I grunted, pushing him again. "Now quit bitching and *move* before someone sees you."

Blaze walked willingly with me for a few feet before whispering, "Her brother is Killian O'Shea. And he was coming to intervene with Kosrath. How did I not see that?"

"You seemed to be staring at our lovely new mate."

His eyes darted to mine, his mouth falling open in shock as he froze in the middle of the hallway. "Shit, she is our mate, isn't she?"

I smiled at the way his voice sounded, all soft and filled with wonder. "Yes, she absolutely is."

"Kosrath is a dead man." His eyes darkened, and the glow from his wolf spirit appeared once more. "How dare he touch what's mine?"

I shoved him into the wall, growling as I pinned him with my body. "Ours."

"Yes. Yes, ours." His hands came up to grip my arms, holding me in place. "We should go—"

"No." I bumped him into the wall again, keeping him there in case he didn't have full control of his wolf. "We cannot go out there and make a scene."

He growled, glaring at me. "Why not?"

"Because it's too public. Every wolf salivating to take your spot would see her as your ultimate weakness, and she'd become their prey. We can't let anyone know you've found a new mate until she moves in to the Fields where we can keep her safe."

Blaze's face fell, all anger and fury bleeding out of him. "Fuck."

"Yeah." Comfortable that he wasn't going to try to blast through me to get to our pretty mate, I used one hand to dig into my pocket for my phone. "She's going to need a guard. I'm calling Bez."

"A Cleaner?" Blaze asked. "Why not call down one of the Feral Breed crews instead?"

"The Cleaners have more firepower should anyone try to snatch her."

"Jesus." Blaze sagged, his head coming to rest on my shoulder. "I've been so busy trying to find her, I never thought about what to do once I did."

"Oh, I've thought about what we're going to do."

Blaze rolled his eyes, a surprisingly modern and immature action for a wolf as aged as he. When my phone pinged, I checked the screen and nodded.

"Bez is on his way down now. He'll confirm once he has her in sight. He's bringing Levi with him to take care of Kosrath."

Blaze nodded, running a palm over his handsome face and dropping his head back against the wall. "I don't want to wait for her."

"I don't either," I replied. "But we need to make sure she's safe before any of the other Alphas figures out what's going on."

Blaze knocked his head back against the wall, still staring at the ceiling. "Fuck, just looking at her made me so hard."

My phone pinged again. I smiled as I read the message from Bez saying he had our mate in view.

Excited, anxious, and turned the fuck on at the prospect of finally completing our triad, I dropped my phone in my pocket and palmed Blaze's erection. "Finally, something I can help you with."

Blaze started to roll his eyes again but quickly stopped. He stared at me, that fire and power he wore so well flowing through him. Finding our mate may have knocked him off his game for a moment, but he was swiftly regaining his control. And when he gave me a sexy smirk, I knew my man was ready to play.

"Get on your knees."

I immediately dropped to the floor, unzipping the fly of his dress pants and pulling him out with practiced ease. "What my mate wants, my mate gets."

With no fanfare, no teasing touches or introductory licks, I sucked his heavy cock into my mouth. All the way in. He groaned as my nose hit his stomach, his hands going to the sides of my head.

"So that's how you're going to be tonight?" he asked, already bucking into my mouth.

I hollowed my cheeks and slid my mouth all the way to the tip before swallowing him back down. Reaching between his legs, I wrapped my fingers around his balls, rolling and tugging on them the way I knew he loved. Fuck answering his silly question; there was no way I was using my mouth for anything other than pleasuring him right then. He needed to come, and I needed to make him.

I bobbed my head at a fast pace, letting Blaze push and pull on me when he chose to. Running my teeth along the bottom of his cock every few strokes, I made sure to suck him deep and hard. He groaned and growled, yanking my hair. As his balls tightened up and his hips jerked, I went against what he wanted. I slowed my pace, still sucking him from base to tip while squeezing his balls. But I also kept one hand flat against his stomach, pushing him against the wall. Holding him in place.

"Fuck, Dante."

I growled, knowing how much he liked the vibrations. His hips jerked, his grunts turning to whimpers as his muscles began to clench. Two more bobs and he came with a gasp. I kept him sucked all the way in, letting him come down my throat as he bit his lip to hold back the roar I knew he wanted to release.

When he was spent, I licked my way back to the head, using the tip of my tongue to play with his foreskin before I gave his cock a quick kiss goodbye. Or, really, a see-you-later. I had a feeling neither of us would be getting any sleep tonight.

"Think she'll like being with the two of us?" Blaze asked as he ran his hands through my hair and over my face. I rose to meet him, kissing him good and deep even as his hand slid into the waistband of my trousers. "I mean, she could be a bit innocent, for all we know."

I rolled my eyes. "That woman is no more innocent than I am; she's practically sex on legs. Besides, I think she'll like whatever we do to her because every action will be for her pleasure."

"I like that thought." He gripped my weeping cock in his hand, running his fingers along me softly, slowly. A casual wander on a Sunday afternoon instead of a rush-hour trip on the expressway.

"Hmmm, I like *this.*" I thrust into his hand and kissed him again. Soft and sweet and filled with a hope we hadn't felt in a long time. "We have a meeting scheduled with her and her brother in the morning, and afterward"—I jerked as his hand sped up—"we'll bring her home with us."

Moving his mouth to my neck, Blaze placed small bites along the length, jacking my cock harder and faster. I shivered, feeling my own orgasm building inside of me.

"Blaze," I whispered, letting my head fall to his shoulder. He growled, fastening his teeth over the claiming mark he'd given me half a millennium ago and biting deep.

I came with a gasp, growling and cursing, pumping my hips

into Blaze's fist. And when I was done, spent in the best possible way, I leaned forward for one more kiss from my mate.

He met my gaze, gave me a peck, and whispered, "Tomorrow."

CHAPTER FIVE

moira

THE HALL WAS DARKER THAN I expected, the shadows dancing across the plush carpet underfoot. I crept along, inwardly cursing my cowardice. I should have just barged down the corridor and confronted the staring men. But even though my mind said, "Go, fight, win," my body refused to obey. Instead, I slunk and skulked like some kind of thief. Perhaps my refusal to act as brash as I knew I normally was had to do with the uncertainty of the odd events in the ballroom. Could one of those men have been my mate? I thought maybe, but it was hard to know for sure. Yes, I'd felt a pull to one of them, but which? And why did he leave and not come to meet me?

Turning a corner, the sound of a hushed argument reached my ears. Or perhaps not an argument. It was too hard to tell the context of the whispered conversation without moving closer, but the possibility of their hearing or catching my scent grew with every step. Slowly, carefully, I inched my way toward the sounds, my hands sweaty and my heart beating so fast, I swore it was about to take flight from my chest.

"Get on your knees."

I nearly gasped as the command rang loud and clear through the darkened hall. Who was back there? Was my mate with another woman? Was he running so as not to have to refuse me in public? My heart broke at the thought, but my backbone didn't. I stood tall and stepped with purpose, ready to confront the coward.

But when I reached the final corner, what I saw made me freeze.

Tall, handsome, and tousled in a way only sexy, charming men could pull off, the light-haired one leaned against the wall, his eyes locked on the face of the darker man. The one kneeling in front of him. The one sucking his dick. Holy hell, I wasn't sure whether to be pissed off or turned on. Or both.

"So that's how you're going to be tonight?"

My knees nearly buckled at the throaty sound of the standing male's voice. The other man responded by bobbing his head faster, his hand disappearing between his partner's legs.

Partner.

Damn it, these two were lovers. Partners. Their scents mingled on the air as I watched them in their intimate moment, the aroma well-mixed and balanced. This was not their first time together, nor were they casual about their relationship. Being that I could still feel the draw of a mating bond to one of them, I had to assume they'd claimed each other outside of their fated matches. The way their scents were joined, the unspoken intimacy between them, how comfortable they seemed together…these two had been a couple for a long time. Which meant I was not needed and possibly not wanted.

The pull to be near whoever was my mate hadn't lessened a bit, but there was no way I was interrupting such a moment. Not to mention I had no desire to be humiliated when told I wasn't wanted by the man my fate had led me to.

"Fuck, Dante."

An uncomfortable itch crept up my spine, a feeling of doing something I shouldn't. Something dirty and rude. Knowing I was in the wrong place, I turned to go back to the ballroom. At least my mate had found someone to be with. And now that I knew, now that the option of joining with my mate was gone, I could move on. Find a wolf to claim as my own. True, my life would be shortened by denying the bond of true mates, but that was a small price to pay for certainty.

Yes, I was better off learning that my mate preferred another this way, and not after meeting him and having to deal with the rejection face-to-face.

Turning another corner, I was knocked literally to a stop by a large shifter in a dark suit. Something about him pushed me past my comfort zone, something dark and edgy about his close-cropped blond hair and his ice-blue eyes. There was an air about him that set my instincts ablaze. He made me want to escape, to run and hide, and yet, I couldn't allow him to happen upon the couple I'd just left. This man was the walking, talking epitome of danger, and my mate was too wrapped up in his… partner…to be prepared.

Pasting on my most dazzling smile—the one that got me everything from extra ice cream at dinner to a reduced fee on a lumber delivery last year—I cocked my hip with a little added vigor.

"Are you lost, honey?"

His eyes zeroed in on mine, flat and bottomless. Soulless.

"No. I'm looking for someone."

I laughed through the ice forming in my heart, the terror his voice instilled in me. "Oh, there's no one back there. I've just come from the end of that hall. I thought the ladies' room would be down there, but I guess not." I grabbed his elbow and began leading him toward the ballroom, ignoring the way he stiffened and growled at my touch. "I can't help thinking this place was designed by someone with no sense of direction.

Every hallway turns and twists and takes you places you don't expect. I just spent ten minutes trying to find a restroom, and instead I found empty hall after empty hall."

The man stared without blinking—making me shiver. *What the hell?*

"Are you sure?" he asked, those freakishly pale eyes locked on mine. "One of the waiters directed me down here for the men's room."

"Oh, I'm sure." I quickened my step, needing to get this man out of the hall and then to get him the hell away from me. "Perhaps the waiter meant the other side of the ballroom. I'm certain there are facilities there."

He chuckled, the sound more mocking than happy. "I guess I'm at your mercy then."

◊ ◊ ◊

Once I'd escaped from the creepy guy in search of the bathroom, I left the ballroom party behind. I pulled off my heels before I even reached the elevator, not caring at the odd looks people gave me. Forget etiquette; my heart had been broken before it even had the chance to be whole, plus, I'd had to spend far too much time in the dark with probably the scariest man I'd ever met. Etiquette could kiss my ass.

When I reached my room, I stripped out of my dress and tossed my shoes across the room. More like threw them, but at this point, I wasn't about to start splitting hairs. My heart raced and my skin itched with a need to shift, all due to the adrenaline pumping through my body. Falling on the bed, I buried my face in my pillow and absolutely refused to think of the men in the hallway. Of how handsome they each seemed to be from what little I saw of them. Of how good they looked together. Of how hot seeing them in such an intimate moment made me.

I groaned and tried to block my thoughts about the way the

kneeling man's head had bobbed on the other's dick. How the groans and messy, wet sounds had teased my ears, making me want to move closer. How, deep down, I wished I could have seen more. I rolled my hips as need blazed low in my belly. It was so wrong to be turned on by what I'd seen, but I couldn't help myself. Those two men had made me wet with desire, and I was too wound up to ignore it.

Sighing, frustrated with myself but surrendering to my desire, I slid one hand between my hips and the mattress, keeping my fingers outside my panties. As if not actually touching my flesh would make this less wrong in some way. And it was wrong. I shouldn't be touching myself thinking of the man leaning against the wall. About the way he stared down at the other, biting his lip and gripping his head. As my fingers sped up, I chastised myself for thinking about the man on his knees. Dante, the other had called him Dante. Just thinking the word made me gasp and moan.

The vigor with which Dante had sucked and bobbed, how he had obviously enjoyed the action, made me positively writhe against the mattress. The way Dante had slid his hand into the other man's pants, so practiced and at ease. This was not something new to either of them, which was a thought that made my legs tremble with a need for release.

Fuck, my fingers had slipped inside my panties of their own volition. My flesh was soaked, my clit swollen. I rubbed harder, making little circles as I practically humped my hand. Frustrated and empty, I worked my other hand around my hip, thrusting two fingers inside my pussy. Better. Oh God, so much better. I pushed and pulled and circled and clenched, my hands working in tandem, my mind replaying the way the standing man had growled when Dante had slid his hand inside his pants. Dante must have grabbed his balls. Or maybe—God, oh God, oh God—Dante had pressed his fingers against the other's asshole and—

I came with a shout, my walls squeezing my fingers and my entire body stiffening. I pressed my hand against my clit, drawing out the orgasm, too sensitive to do more than just apply pressure. And when I was finished, when I was physically spent from masturbating but still tied up inside, I turned over and huffed.

Stupid handsome wolves and their stupid probably-just-as-handsome lovers and their ridiculously hot blow jobs. How was I supposed to keep myself from getting turned on by such a sight? And if that was what they were willing to do in public, the thought of what they would be doing alone in their room…

I shuffled off the bed and headed to the bathroom, needing a shower. And maybe a few moments with the removable shower head. One more time getting off to thoughts of what I couldn't have, and then I would move on with my life. There was a lot of business left to accomplish in the morning before I headed home. Alone.

Chapter Six

dante

I GRIPPED THE EDGE OF the podium with sweaty hands. This was it. The O'Sheas were due in the presidential chamber in a matter of minutes. Blaze and I would need to act unaffected by our mate, but afterward…

Well, afterward, I was hoping for us to be really affected by our mate. Multiple times. In more positions than I could count.

Not that all either of us could think about was sex. Finding the third to our triad was a momentous event, bringing someone else into our relationship to love and pamper and protect, something to celebrate. But honestly, after seeing her last night in the ballroom, we'd both been ridiculously turned on. We'd spent the hours after the party going back and forth, taking and giving in every conceivable way until we finally fell into a heap on the floor and passed out. But today was a new day, and we were energized and ready to claim the final piece to the puzzle of our destiny.

I smelled her before I heard her, heard her before I saw her, and knew Blaze was fighting to remain impassive and stoic before she entered the room. This would be a true test for him. He couldn't let the sneaky fuckers see his weakness. We'd hoped the meeting room would be empty this morning, the Gathering participants too worn out from the previous night's celebration to attend. But we'd been unpleasantly surprised when two regional heads walked through the doors to witness the proceedings. We, and especially Blaze, would need to keep our hands close to the vest today. At least until we got Moira alone.

She walked in with her brother, the two of them quite an impressive pair of shifter genetics. Both tall and dark, they exuded a confidence that was envious. But when I looked closely, because of course I was inspecting every inch of my newfound mate, I could see the tells of her nerves. The way her thumb ran over the tip of her fingers. How the muscles in her neck pulled tight. The slight flush to her chest. Yes, she was nervous. And that nervousness threatened to explode the moment she saw Blaze.

Her breath caught and her eyes went wide when Blaze looked her way, as if she recognized him or felt the mating pull to him. A sting of jealousy burned but only for a moment. I knew she'd look at me the same way once our eyes locked. She couldn't help it; the bond the fates created was a powerful force.

"I'd like to introduce Alpha Killian O'Shea from the Southern Appalachia pack, along with his Alpha female, Moira O'Shea." I nodded to the pair as I stepped away from the podium, leaving room for Blaze to take his rightful place and waiting for the moment when Moira swung her eyes my way. It took longer than I would have liked, but finally, finally, she glanced at me. And my world went sideways.

Beautiful, dark eyes met mine, accentuated by the rosy flush of her cheeks. Her breaths came faster, making me want to drop my eyes to her chest. To watch as those full breasts moved with each respiration. But I refrained. I held her gaze as confusion and fear danced across her features. Willing her to figure it out, to understand why she felt so drawn to both Blaze and me.

Her eyes darted to Blaze, back to me, to Blaze again. Fear led to panic, fast breathing led to near-silent gasping. She was going to run. I tried to hold her gaze even as I chanted pleas in my head, wishing there were some way to let Blaze know what was coming. She didn't understand yet, didn't realize she'd been bonded into a triad. All she knew was she felt the pull to her fated mate with Blaze, and then with me. And she was afraid.

But then her eyes grew even wider and her flush deepened. I could practically see the wheels turning in her mind as she figured it out, gaze still darting back and forth from me to Blaze. And when she finally stopped, when she stared at me with her mouth agape, I answered her unspoken question with a simple head nod and a small lift to the corner of my mouth.

Minutes passed as Blaze and Killian spoke politics and land allotments. The new Alpha had a keen sense for business, but I paid him little mind. Instead, I kept my eyes on a very introspective-looking Moira, giving her silly smiles and heated looks as I waited for the drone of the NALB leader to conclude.

"Welcome to the NALB, Alpha Killian," Blaze said, his words finally making sense in my head. This was it. We were so close to being done. "I was about to retire to my suite for brunch. I extend an invitation for you to join me. And your lovely sister, of course."

His words were crisp and professional, but I knew my mate. Knew the way he gripped the side of the podium was a sign of his tension. Knew he wanted to host Killian O'Shea about as much as I did. Not that we had any problem with the new Alpha, but he stood in the way of some serious conversations and possible not-conversations with our mate.

Luckily for us, Killian balked at the invitation before he was able to school his features. "Uh, well, you see—"

"Oh, of course." Blaze smiled his NALB-president smile, the one that never quite reached his eyes. "You found your mate while here. Congratulations."

"Thank you."

"I do understand the undeniable draw to a new fated union." His gaze flickered to Moira, a tiny move he quickly corrected. Still, I tensed as I glanced toward the regional heads. Neither seemed to be paying attention to the goings-on, which was good. If one of them should find out about Blaze's tie to Moira, the rest of the bastards would know within minutes, and she would definitely be in danger.

Killian swallowed and ran a hand through his hair. "Yes, well, while I appreciate the invitation—"

"Say no more." Blaze waved his hand, glancing down at his papers as if he were looking for information. I tried not to smile, knowing the move for what it was. Blaze's chance to disseminate all the sensory input from the room and get his words in order. To scent the room, to concentrate on the energy around him, and to hear more than what was being said before he made his case known. The man was nothing if not deliberate.

When he raised his eyes, he looked right at Moira. "Perhaps your sister would care to join me. I would like to discuss the cultivation of the maple trees on your land. I realize sugaring isn't a large-income endeavor, but I have a bit of a soft spot for all things…sweet."

Killian looked to his sister, shocking me. That move was a sign of weakness in a man with his kind of power. He should have made the decision for his packmate, even if it upset Moira. The regional heads practically salivated at the display, sending a chill up my spine. We needed to get Moira out of here, away from these men, before they began propositioning her and blowing our charade. A woman in power was practically an aphrodisiac to our breed, and Killian had just outed Moira as a woman with more power than even he held.

Moira nodded to Blaze as she clasped her hands in front of her. "I would be honored, sir."

I nearly growled at the sound of her voice, but I managed to bite it back. Blaze appeared to be struggling with his reaction to her as well. He shuffled his papers and kept his eyes down as he said quietly, "Yes, wonderful. We'll have a nice brunch before the afternoon meetings."

"May I have a moment of your time, President Zenne?" one of the regional heads asked. A particularly old shifter with a bad attitude and even worse breath, he also seemed to have the worst sense of timing in the universe. Knowing Blaze was at the end of his tether, I stood, practically creating a barrier between the two.

"You may have fifteen minutes at the start of the afternoon session, but Blasius will not be rude to his guest by delaying their meal." I turned and winked at Blaze before stepping off the dais and heading to Moira. Breathing her in, fighting back a growl at her honey and cinnamon scent, I held out a hand for her.

"Will you please come with me?"

A simple question, in theory, but practically earth-shattering in context. I wanted her. Just as much as I wanted Blaze. I wanted to pull her into my arms and kiss her throat. Wanted to run my fingers through her thick, dark hair, using it as a handhold to arch her body as I slid into her from behind. Wanted to give her my mating bite as Blaze did the same.

But first, I had to convince her to simply take my hand.

She glanced at the proffered body part, a bit of anxiety keeping her from reaching for me. Confident in her response, I smiled and waited. When she finally took a deep breath and placed her hand in mine, my smile turned to a grin.

Heart racing but light, mind positively spinning, I led her across the floor and out the door, Blaze following closely behind us. A growl rumbled from his chest, low and constant, but definitely loud enough for Moira to hear. And by the way her body was reacting, she did; something between fear and excitement making her tremble.

"Good morning, gentlemen. And, ma'am." Bez, Moira's personal guard for the time being, nodded as he stepped in front of our group, a small lift of the lips on his normally impassive face. Moira started and stared, having obviously run into the man before.

The soldier led the way to our suite, opening the door and ushering us inside.

"Thank you, Bez," Blaze said as he crossed the threshold. "We'll let you know when you're needed."

"Of course, sir." Before the big man could close the door, Blaze stopped it with a hand.

"And I expect a full report of what this"—Blaze motioned between the guard and Moira—"is all about."

The man practically grinned, his ice-blue eyes darting to our new mate. And then he winked at her. "Yes, sir, though it's a short story. Just two people who ended up down the wrong hallway as we were each looking for a restroom."

He closed the door behind him, a husky chuckle echoing in the hall. Moira stared after him for a moment, looking slightly confused. But she shook that off quickly and crossed to the balcony doors, staring out the window. For several minutes, none of us said a single word. Each waiting on another to start the conversation we all needed to have. Figures it was our mate who was the one brave enough to do it.

"What is this?"

"This what?" Blaze asked, his voice tight as he moved toward her.

She turned, her glare pinning Blaze where he stood. "This everything. What's happening here?"

Blaze looked at me as if for help, so I shrugged and chose the path of least resistance.

"You're our mate," I said. "Our third."

Moira scoffed. "That's not possible. Only the strongest wolves end up in triads."

I raised an eyebrow. "Are you questioning our strength?"

She faltered for a moment before squaring her shoulders. "No, I'm questioning my own."

Blaze laughed, finally relaxing as he crossed to the bar cabinet. "Darling, you shouldn't underestimate yourself. We just watched as your Alpha, the leader of your pack and a strong male wolf spirit, deferred to you when we asked you to join us."

"Of course he did," she replied, looking at him as if he were crazy. "Killian would never make me go where I didn't want to be."

"But any other Alpha in this building would." Blaze handed our woman a glass of wine before walking over and giving me my own. I kissed his cheek and whispered my thanks. Moira took a sip of the dark red liquid, watching our interaction. Evaluating us.

"Do you not drink?" she asked.

"Not when I have to attend business meetings later, no." Blaze moved closer to her, his steps light. A hunter stalking his prey in a dark suit and dress shoes. "I prefer to keep my instincts and reflexes sharp. It's safer that way."

She blinked at him. "Safer?"

"Did you see the two older shifters in the seats to your right?" I asked, flanking Blaze, trapping her between us. "One of them asked for Blaze's attention."

She nodded.

"The one with the darker hair has been plotting different ways to oust Blaze and take over as head of the NALB for almost a decade." I inched closer, stopping when she took a step back. "The other likes to try to undermine every ruling Blaze issues to show him as an incompetent leader. Two paths to the same destination—they want the presidency."

"But surely they're not dangerous?" She took another step back, my nearness obviously making her nervous.

I sighed and downed my wine, moving past her as I headed

to the bar for a second glass. "Nearly every NALB president has been murdered while in office. All but one—the man Blaze succeeded."

Moira turned her attention to our mate. "You didn't kill him?"

"No," Blaze answered. "I liked the old bastard. Instead of killing him, I outmaneuvered him."

"How?"

Blaze smiled. "That's a story for another time. For now, just know that there is always danger at my door, a door I'm hoping you'll be behind with us soon."

"And Officer Creepy out there?" Moira asked, gesturing toward the door with her glass.

"You mean Bez?" I asked. "Don't worry about him. He's there to protect you."

"Protect *me*?" Moira asked, raising her eyebrows.

"Of course." Blaze approached her once more, keeping his body language soft and unthreatening. "Sweet girl, when we saw you last night, we knew you were our mate."

Moira's face fell, as if that was the last thing she wanted to hear. "You knew last night?"

"Of course we did," I replied. I wished I could read her mind, know why her voice sounded suddenly so sad, so disappointed. "But there's always danger lurking. If we had acted on our desperation to be close to you in the middle of that damned party, every NALB regional head would've known. They would've seen how much you meant to Blaze, and you would've become the ultimate bait."

Moira shook her head. "I don't understand."

"They want his spot," I explained. "They'll exploit any weakness they can find to get it. I'm a weakness; you're a weakness. The difference between the two of us is that I'm always either with Blaze and his Cleaners or under guard. You're here on your own."

She bristled. "My pack is with me."

Blaze shook his head, watching her carefully. "These men have annihilated entire packs to take over their territories. They wouldn't be stopped by doors and locks and a handful of shifters."

"So you live in fear?" she asked.

"No, never fear." Blaze shook his head, moving closer to her, dropping his voice to a softer level. "Irritation. Frustration. Exhaustion. But never fear."

"That's why you left the ballroom," she said, eyebrows raised again. "To keep me out of danger."

"Yes. We needed privacy before we could tell you about us… our bond." Blaze glanced at me, confusion clear in the way his brows furrowed. I shrugged and waited for something to help me figure out where this conversation was going.

Instead of talking, Moira moved about the room, drinking from her glass as her fingers glided over tables and decorator items, only stopping when she reached a picture frame on the console table. I knew the picture well; it was my favorite. One I never left Merriweather Fields without. Taken a mere three years ago at a Feral Breed meeting, Blaze and I lounged at the bar. Blaze's arm around my waist, my head thrown back as I laughed at something our friend Jameson had said. That had been a good day. A fun day. But Moira looked sad as she inspected it. Almost wistful.

"I saw you," she whispered, setting the picture back on the table.

Blaze's head jerked back. "Pardon?"

"Last night in the hallway," she whispered.

Blaze glanced at me as my stomach sank, his eyes wide, showing the same level of unease that seemed to be resting on my chest.

"When you left the ballroom, I followed." Moira looked up, her eyes meeting mine. Wary…uncertain. "I saw the two of you together."

I held her gaze, not understanding the sad tone in her voice. "I'm not sure where you're going with this. Do you…not approve of the two of us being together?"

"Oh God, no," she said in a rush. "Seeing the two of you together was…well, not a bad thing. But I'm curious. How would it work?"

Blaze's eyebrows shot up. "How would what work?"

"This," she said with a shrug. "Us. The three of us. I saw you two…together. How would we work with three?"

I chuckled, finally catching on to her fear. "The same as with two. There'd just be…more options."

She gave me a mock-frown, but a devilish glint in her eye belied her true feelings. "Be serious."

"I'm completely serious." I stepped closer, my body craving nearness and connection to her. "Let it be known, I never joke about sex."

"He doesn't," Blaze said in his most deadpan business tone. "He really doesn't."

She rolled her eyes. "You two have obviously been together a long time."

"Five hundred years—"

"You can tell that by how I blow him?" Blaze and I spoke at once, turning to glare at one another's interruptions. Moira laughed, the sound drawing our attention.

"First, yes. I can tell that from the way you blew him." She grinned all cocky and proud as we gaped at her. "There was an intimacy between the two of you that only comes with time. And five hundred years is a long time to be together, just the two of you." She looked down, her voice growing softer. "I'd hate to be in the way."

Blaze and I exchanged a look before we rushed to her, caging her between us, the energy sparking as the three of us came in contact for the first time.

"You're our mate," I said. "The final piece to our triad puzzle."

Blaze growled. "You would never be in the way."

Moira glanced from one of us to the other, questioning. We didn't move, didn't blink as we waited on her decision. She must have found the answers she needed because, in the next minute, all traces of the anxious woman disappeared. In her place stood the brazen shewolf who'd swept across the dance floor the night before and kicked an Alpha in the balls. Confident, calm, and incredibly sexy.

"So," she said, drawing out the single syllable. "You want me?"

"Yes." Blaze and I spoke at once, our answer immediate and definitive.

"Both of you?" She raised her eyebrows again as the corners of her mouth lifted.

"Yes," I replied.

"Absolutely," Blaze answered.

She gave me a heated once-over. "He gave you orders, and you followed them."

I growled, sensing something changing on the air. Some kind of heat and tension growing between the three of us. "I like when he's bossy."

She stuck out her bottom lip in the sexiest little mock-pout known to man. "What if I like to be the one in charge?"

CHAPTER SEVEN

dante

I GROWLED AND STALKED MY mate, loving the way she teased, that pout morphing into a sassy smile and making me even harder. Blaze circled from her other side, the heated look on his face and the bulge behind the fly of his trousers sure signs he was on the same page as I was.

I nearly grunted as her eyes met mine, desperate to touch her. "Does that mean you might accept us, be willing to enter into our triad as the fates prescribed?"

Moira shrugged, trying to remain aloof, but I could smell the desire on her. Could see the need burning bright in those dark eyes of hers. She liked the idea of the three of us together just as much as Blaze and I did.

"Perhaps," she whispered, not that the volume mattered. We were inches away, standing so close I could have reached for Blaze's hands and completely caged her in.

Moira shivered as we inched closer, her body responding so well to us. Her nipples stood tall and proud under her blouse, screaming for my lips and tongue. Damn, I wanted to touch her, to taste her. A growl thrummed out of me, a tone of longing. Blaze joined me, his longer and louder than my own, his wolf spirit needing to show its dominance to me. Not that I minded. I loved when Blaze threw off the proper businessman facade and let himself surrender to his more primal urges. And right then, I'd have bet every dime I had that those urges were centered on claiming our mate.

"And what could we do to convince you, dear Moira?" Blaze asked, his voice rough, low, and deep. The tone sent shivers up my spine and made Moira gasp. I wanted to tell her how amazing we could make her feel, how she'd tremble and quake under our touch. But some people learn better by doing than hearing, so I took a deep breath and closed the gap between us.

Gripping her hips, sighing as my cock met the softness of her stomach, I pulled her in tight against me. Blaze mimicked my actions, hands on her waist as he pressed against her back, still growling for her. She didn't jump or pull away, just met my hungry gaze and put her hands on my arms. Clinging to me already.

"Tell us, my dove," I said as I ran my nose along her cheek and toward her ear. "What can we do to have you give us a chance?"

I licked her earlobe before moving back, watching her for any sign of refusal. Her head lolled back against Blaze's chest as he licked the length of her neck, her eyes closing at the sensation. Her hands moved up and down my arms, rubbing me, enticing me. I did her one better, sliding my hands around her hips, cupping her ass. The back of one hand brushed across Blaze's cock. He jerked and met my gaze over her shoulder, his eyes glowing with need. I massaged her ass, rubbing and squeezing that succulent flesh, teasing him as much as I was teasing her.

Eyes on Blaze's, I leaned down and brushed my nose against hers. "Tell me what you need."

She lifted her head, meeting my eyes and giving me a

fantastically sexy growl. "More."

"More of what?" I asked as Blaze's hands moved up her ribs. "More of me? Of him? Of us together?"

"Yes." She gasped when Blaze cupped her breasts, shivered when he pinched her nipples through her blouse. "Oh, yes to all of it. Yes."

Had I not been pressing my cock against the stomach of my now groaning female mate, I would have punched the air in victory. Instead, I met the eyes of the man I'd been in love with for five centuries. "What do you think, Blaze?"

"I think we should give the lady what she wants." One corner of his mouth tipped up, but his eyes were filled with the soul of his wolf. I got the message loud and clear, understating exactly how dominant my lover was.

Moira gasped as he tweaked her nipples and bit her shoulder. The bite wasn't a claiming one as it wasn't hard enough to break the skin, but it was a good indicator of what he wanted to do. Blaze kept his eyes on mine as he took a step back, pulling Moira with him. I nodded and let my hands slide from her ass. Moira's eyes locked on mine, her desire almost making me whimper, but it was the question I saw there that made me smile.

"I'm going to let Blaze take the lead this first time, dove," I said as Blaze slid a hand into her pants. She pressed back against him, spreading her legs a little, enjoying whatever he was doing to her. "Don't worry, though. I'll be watching and learning."

I took a seat on the couch as Blaze wrapped himself around our mate. One hand up her blouse, the other in her pants, both working in ways that made her hips writhe and her eyes close. Face buried in her neck, Blaze sank to the floor, taking her with him. The sight of them on their knees that way made me practically insane with lust. The position, the contradiction of their clothing and their actions. Her arms up and clutching the back of his head, that cream silk blouse with the little pearl buttons pulling out of the waistband of her gray dress pants. His suit disheveled, the dark, pinstriped fabric contrasting with her pale skin and blouse as his arms moved underneath. Beautiful, sexy…some kind of naughty workplace fantasy coming to life before my eyes.

Blaze laid Moira down, sliding his long body on top of hers, fitting between her thighs as she spread her legs for him. I palmed my cock through my trousers, my eyes locked on the sight before me. Kissing deeply, hands roaming, and tongues sliding together, my two mates had my utmost attention. Soft moans and rumbling growls soon joined the wet sounds of their kissing, the groans as they rubbed their bodies together. Watching them made my heart happy, but it also drove me past the point of lust and desire to full-on sexual need. As Blaze rutted against our mate, I unzipped my trousers, freeing myself from behind the ridiculous fabric. My fingers curved expertly around my cock, the touch making me shiver. It wasn't what I wanted, not even close, but it would have to do. For now.

I stroked up, tugging on the foreskin before sliding my hand back down. My eyes locked on the way Blaze undulated against Moira; the way the two of them fit together so perfectly. I could almost see myself with them, exactly where I'd fit in that picture. Almost feel the heat from our three bodies pressed together. Biting my lip, craving and waiting and wanting, I kept my hand moving in time with them. Running a thumb over the tip on every upstroke. Lifting my hips to thrust into my fist on the downstroke. Participating the only way I could. Blaze, as the more dominant in our triad, would claim Moira first. But then she'd be mine; they both would. Mine to hold and caress, to worship and taste, to lick and suck and experience whatever fantasy we could dream up. And eventually, once we'd spent a good amount of time preparing her for it, we'd take her at the same time. Filling her completely. Fuck, the thought made me whimper.

Moira must have heard me because she turned her head

and met my gaze. Blaze pressed up on his arms, giving me a view that made my balls tingle. Moira, on the floor underneath him, looking so fucking sexy and disheveled. Long, dark hair all mussed, blouse unbuttoned, lacy bra cups pulled under her breasts, exposing them, her dark nipples hard and begging to be tugged. To be licked. Bitten.

Blaze shot me a look that screamed sex as he dropped his head, wrapping his lips around her nipple, sucking as he kept his gaze on mine. My hand moved faster, a whimpered groan escaping as I watched. Wishing to be closer, wanting to taste what Blaze was.

Surprising the both of us, Moira wriggled out from under Blaze and rose to her knees. Blaze followed, coming up behind her and looking over her shoulder. She turned just enough to give him a long, deep kiss before looking my way again as she slowly stripped out of her clothes. Blouse and bra tossed to the side, she stood to push her pants off her hips as Blaze gripped her hips and nibbled the curve of her waist. When she was naked—completely, confidently, stunningly naked—she walked to me while holding out a hand to Blaze.

"We're three, right?" she asked, her eyes locked on mine.

"Yes." My hand stopped, though my fingers still held my cock, my thumb occasionally sliding over the tip.

Moira dropped her eyes to my lap, cocking her head as she watched my fingers squeeze, my thumb swipe. Looking deliciously aroused and desirous. "So then our first claiming should be as three, yes?"

Blaze sat back on his heels, his hard cock pointing to the ceiling as he rubbed his face on her hip. "But my sweet, there are physical demands of mating as three. You're not prepared for that."

"Who's to say?" Moira ran her fingers through his hair, the confidence and challenge in her gaze making my cock weep and my growl rumble. "Perhaps having two men inside of me is something I've done before."

As Blaze stared, looking completely shocked, I sat back and gave her a smirk. Our girl seemed to be a little on the dirty side, which I liked. A lot. Moira smiled back at me and strutted to the couch, pushing my shoulders until she had me adjusted the way she wanted. Leaning back against the arm, practically lying along the length. As Blaze watched, she stripped me, quick and efficient, pulling my shirt over my head and my pants down while I lay there, completely at her mercy.

"Blaze, baby?" she asked, glancing over her shoulder. "Strip for your mates, please."

Blaze grinned, quickly undressing himself while the two of us watched. She moaned when she saw him fully naked, her hand sliding to her own breast to pull on her nipple. Our mate was a sexy beast, powerful and lithe, with long, lean muscles. He wasn't bulky like a lot of shifters, his physical strength being far less obvious than some. But like this, bare and proud and standing before us, there was no denying who was the strongest shifter in the room.

"You want us to claim you at the same time?" Blaze growled, coming to her side. Moira nodded, still staring at the wonder of our mate. I reached for her hand, capturing her attention.

"Have you had sex with two men at once?" I yanked on her arm, suddenly craving the feel of her skin against mine. "Have you had one cock in your ass while another was deep inside your pussy?"

She didn't answer right away, instead moving to join me on the couch. My eyes nearly rolled back as she climbed on top of me, straddling my hips, running her hot pussy along my length. When I groaned, she grinned and leaned down to bite my lip.

"No." She glanced at Blaze as my heart sank in disappointment. I'd liked the idea of our first time, our first coupling, being complete. The possibility of claiming her as triads were meant to, with synchronized bites, had been a dream I hadn't dared to hope for until she mentioned it. But apparently we'd have to wait for—

"But I've had anal sex more times than I can count, so handling the two of you really shouldn't be an issue."

My eyes darted to Blaze, my eyebrows high. Fuck me, was she serious? Blaze blinked twice, his face devoid of expression. But then a very devilish glint appeared in his eye and one corner of his mouth tipped up.

"Are you sure?" he asked, his voice barely more than a growl.

Moira dropped her head back, rubbing herself along my cock. I closed my eyes, consumed by my need for her, wanting so much to slide inside the wet heat she was teasing me with.

"I assume you have…supplies?" she asked.

My eyes popped open in time to see her smile at Blaze. He nodded, looking about as stunned and turned on as I felt.

"I suggest you get them." She rocked her hips against me, coating me in her wetness, grinding down on my cock. I gripped her hips and groaned.

"Fuck, Moira."

She leaned down and bit my bottom lip, just a nip. "You can fuck Moira in a minute." Sitting back up, she sighed and ran her hands over my chest. This time, when she spoke, her voice was soft, her tone no longer filled with confidence. "If we're going to do this, I think we should do it right. While seeing you and Blaze together turned me on, it was also hurtful. I felt almost abandoned watching the two of you and not being able to join in. I don't want either of you to feel that way."

"Dove." I pulled her close as Blaze dropped a bottle of lube and a towel on the floor, looking concerned. "You felt abandoned?"

"Completely. But I understand why you couldn't come to me last night. Really, I do." She sat up, once again pressing her pussy against me in a delicious way. "But it was so hot. I couldn't even think of sleep before I'd come three times last night. I could barely keep my hands out of my pussy."

Blaze's eyes went wide. "Holy hell."

"So how are we doing this?" she asked, glancing from one to the other.

I looked to Blaze, always deferring to him. His eyes were glued to her ass, telling me more than words could.

"I think the current setup's a go, dove."

"Good." She reached for Blaze, grabbing his hips and pulling him close. When she had him where she wanted him, she reached between us and gripped my cock, positioning me at her entrance. I bit my lip as she slid down on me, watching her take Blaze into her mouth at the same time. Fuck, so hot, so wet and tight. The sensation of her wrapped around me while watching as she sucked off our mate was almost too much to bear. I bucked into her, lifting her, making her moan. Blaze must have liked the vibration around his cock because he wove his fingers into her hair and bit his lip, his eyes completely focused on where her lips wrapped around his cock.

"Fuck, sweet girl." Blaze bit his lip and threw his head back, pumping his hips, practically fucking her mouth. I sank back into the couch, letting her ride me in a slow, rocking motion, watching with hungry eyes and loving the way they worked together. The way her lips looked around his cock. Knowing exactly what she was tasting and feeling. I was an expert when it came to Blaze, knowing every dip and ridge. But this was her first time with him, and she was only just learning.

"Use your teeth," I whispered. "He comes so hard when I do that."

Moira moaned, adjusting her jaw and pulling on his hips. Blaze shivered and groaned, his fingers tightening in her hair, his hips moving faster. I matched their rhythm, rocking her over me as she swallowed him down.

"Stop," Blaze gasped after only a few more strokes. "I want to come inside you."

Moira pulled back, looking up at him with a coy grin as she licked his tip a few times for good measure. Blaze leaned down to give her a searing kiss before reaching for the bottle of lube. Moira refocused her attention on me, still rocking as her pussy clutched my cock. Still slow. So fucking slow.

"You're teasing me," I murmured. Moira's eyes closed when Blaze moved behind her, his eyes on her ass as he poured lube over his fingers.

"Just a little bit." She leaned down to kiss me, her lips soft, her tongue searching as it stroked against mine. I cradled her to me, needing to feel her skin against mine, loving the way her soft breasts pressed into my chest. The position also gave Blaze plenty of room to do all that he needed to so he could make sure she was ready to take him. This wasn't the first time we'd shared a woman, though Moira would be the last woman we invited into our bed. Our triad was complete, and we would soon exchange mating bites. She would be ours…forever.

Moira groaned as Blaze licked his lips, her eyes wide and her grip on me tight. I held her in place, keeping her supported as she experienced the first sensations of being filled in both holes. Damn, I couldn't wait to see her come, but I didn't want anything to hurt her. She'd need to be good and ready before Blaze could make a move. To help her, I slid a hand between us, stroking her clit at a slow pace. Just enough to keep her on edge. After a few minutes of this, of growling at every one of her tiny gasps and grunts, Blaze met my eyes and nodded. He reached for the lube, coating his cock with it before he grabbed hold of her hips.

"You're sure, sweet girl?" he asked. She groaned what sounded like a yes, making me chuckle. I lifted her head from my chest, smiling at the way her eyes were unfocused and her mouth hung open.

"Are you ready for us, my mate?" I whispered. She nodded, trembling in my arms. I angled my hips, pulling almost all the way out of her pussy, and nodded to Blaze. He pushed inside slowly, the length of his cock pressing along the tip of mine through the thin wall separating us. I growled and forced my hips to be still as he worked his way in deeper, knowing I had to wait, no matter how much I wanted to bury myself in her. Blaze spent plenty of time nudging his way inside, rocking in and out at a languorous pace. Moira pushed back against Blaze's intrusion, angling her hips, her body begging for more. Her movements had me biting my lip, my arms shaking as I held myself back from thrusting. Fuck, I wanted to be deep inside her. Wanted that heat wrapped around me again.

I knew the moment Blaze seated himself fully inside her. His head dropped back and his fingers curved on her hips, fingertips shifting into claws before he could control it. He held still and growled as I watched, waiting. Dying to move. Dying to slip back inside. When his head came forward and his glowing eyes met mine, I nearly breathed a sigh of relief.

I thrust my hips, pulling my fingers away from her pussy to grip Blaze's hands on her hips, sliding back inside her as he pulled out. The two of us working in opposite directions at the same speed, never pushing her too far or too fast. Not that she seemed to be having any trouble taking us both. She sighed and moaned as she pushed herself up against my chest, angling her hips, her fingernails clawing down my pecs. I loved seeing her this way, all wanton and reduced to nothing but sensation. The pleasure had to be intense for her, the feeling of being filled undeniable.

Minutes passed, Blaze and I watching each other, our fingers tangled on our new mate's hips, our cocks inside her as she moaned and chanted her approval. But then her walls fluttered, her body writhing between us. Our sweet dove wanted to come, was close to that release. I nodded to Blaze, letting him know she was ready, and the two of us sped up our movements. We kept our eyes on our mate, looking for any reaction, making sure we gave her exactly what she needed to come. Releasing my hand, Blaze slid his arm between Moira and me, probably reaching for her clit. The feel of her squeezing my cock, of Blaze's hand moving to where we were joined, was enough to make me groan, fighting back my orgasm. We had to make her come first, needed her to be sated before we could go.

Growling, swearing, grunting, Moira jerked between us, biting my chest as her pleasure grew. Not a mating bite, not yet. But soon. So fucking soon. And I wanted it; I wanted her teeth in me badly. Wanted her to claim me as hers.

"Gonna…oh God…gonna." She shivered and gasped as her pussy locked down on my cock, bringing on my own orgasm as she came around me. Blaze lost his rhythm, jerking his hips against her and following us soon after, his snarl loud. As Moira clenched and growled and moaned with the force of her orgasm, Blaze and I moved in to kiss her neck, licking down the length to the curve of her shoulders.

And then we bit her.

Moira screamed, long and loud and filled with pleasure. The sound and the rush of her spirit toward mine made me experience a second orgasm, something that'd never happened before. I pumped my hips, whimpering, every inch of my body tingling. Blaze pulled out of her with a roar, practically collapsing on top of her as he lapped at the claiming mark he'd left on her neck. She lay still between us, hanging on to us both, panting against my chest. I sighed, one hand tangled in Blaze's hair, the other securely fastened to her hip. Clutching them to me. Relishing in the energy of the triad.

"Bite him," Blaze whispered, sliding down to nibble the back of her shoulder. "I want to watch. Claim him, Moira."

She lifted her head, her unfocused eyes meeting mine even as she spoke to Blaze. "What about you?"

Blaze paused, his voice tinged with apology when he spoke. "I have more meetings to attend and can't do that smelling of you. I want to have you claim me—fuck, do I want you to—but I won't put you in that kind of danger; not yet. I'll get my turn later tonight, but for now, I want to see you take him. He's been waiting a long time for you."

I licked up her chin, sliding my tongue against hers as our lips met. Just for a minute, a short kiss. And then I glanced at Blaze and whispered, "We both have."

Moira leaned down, placing soft kisses up my sternum to my collarbone. She licked my neck as I groaned, nibbled her way across my shoulder as I shivered. And as I hardened again inside of her, rocking my hips in my renewed need to quench my desire for her, she bit me on my pec, right over my heart. Quick, clean, and efficient. Just as I would have expected.

"Fuck, baby." I threw my head back. Thrusting up into her at a brutal pace, my third orgasm slamming into me like none before. Blaze stared at the spot where her teeth met my flesh with glowing eyes, his teeth once again embedded in Moira's neck. Claiming the claimer, the three of us connected. We stayed like that for minutes or hours, no longer caring about time. I had both my mates on top of me, Blaze's eyes on mine, my cock inside Moira's warm pussy, and her teeth in my chest. I was claimed, utterly and completely claimed. My life was quite honestly perfect.

◊ ◊ ◊

After a quick shower to sadly wash our new mate's scent from him, Blaze left with a few soft kisses and a promise to hurry back. Moira and I lay on the floor in front of a fire, naked and snuggling together under a blanket. Yet, for the first time in a number of years, I missed Blaze. I'd long since gotten used to his crazy schedule and the demands his job put on him, but this was different. Tonight, there was a true emptiness inside of me.

"When will he be back?" Moira asked, sounding as lost as I

felt.

"A few hours, I hope."

She whimpered, snuggling closer. "I don't like this."

I kissed her neck, licking over the mark Blaze had left a mere hour ago. "I don't either, but it's his job."

"Will it always be like this? Will there always be danger and guards and rushing out the door for meetings?"

I sighed. "For a few more years at least. Hopefully, he'll decide on a successor and groom that shifter for the seat. That would circumvent the chance of an assassination attempt."

"No one will get close to him," she growled, reminding me of her strength, her inherent power and confidence.

"We'll both make sure of that."

Moira turned in my arms, her face a mix of happiness and anxiety. "I'm going to have to leave my pack."

I pushed a lock of hair behind her ear, knowing she needed my honesty. "Yes, there's no option for you to stay."

She rolled, pulling me on top of her, gripping my hips as I settled between her legs. "I'll never go back there, will I?"

I kissed her, softening my words as much as I could with my affection. "Not for a long time, my dove."

She reached between us and circled her fingers around my cock, her eyes locked on mine. Showing me her fear, her sadness, and her vulnerability.

"Please," she said as she ran the head of my cock along her opening. "I don't want to feel this sad right now."

"I'm sorry," I whispered as I nudged my way inside, resting my forehead against hers. When I was all the way in, my cock deep inside the warmth of her pussy, I held still and clutched her to me. Sighing as she clung to me in return. Doing everything I could to fill her, fill the void Blaze had left when he walked out the door.

As I pulled out and began the long, deep thrusts I sensed she needed, I whispered, "I know this is a lot to handle."

She nodded, wrapping her arms around my shoulders and lifting her hips to meet mine. "It is. But I want it. I want the two of you. There's no question about that; I just didn't realize how strongly I would feel for you both so soon, and how fast things would change."

"We'll get you through it," I said, closing my eyes as the need to come overwhelmed me. She held on to my shoulders and matched my movements, giving as good as I did, the two of us coming together with mingled gasps and groans before collapsing into a sweaty heap on the floor. "You have the two of us. Forever."

CHAPTER EIGHT

moira

Saying goodbye to Killian may have been the hardest thing I'd had to do in my life. I shed a lot of tears as I clung to him, Dante standing nearby with his arm around Killian's new mate. The fact that my brother had met Lyra was the only thing keeping me from begging my men to move to North Carolina—I knew Lyra would take care of Killian. She'd already promised take care of my family and friends.

"I can't believe you're part of a triad," Killian said, refusing to release me from his grasp.

"I can't either, but it's true."

He sighed and whispered, "Are you happy?"

Still missing Blaze, who had yet to return from his meetings, I had to search a little deeper for the truth in my feelings. Was I happy? Yes. No life was easy, and one with a man as powerful as Blaze was sure to bring with it strife and stress. But all in all, my heart was light, my soul was settled, and there was nowhere I wanted to be except with my two men.

"Blissfully," I finally answered, grinning at Dante as he

winked at me.

"That's the last of the bags," Gideon said as he came in carrying my suitcases with Kalie in tow. I pulled myself from my brother's arms and rushed to him, needing one more hug goodbye. He welcomed me with open arms and a smile.

"You take care of that mate of yours, you hear?" I said against his shoulder.

"I will. And you do the same…for both of them."

I felt Blaze approaching before I heard him, opening my eyes to search him out. "I'll do my very best."

Blaze grinned at me as he quickened his pace. I pulled myself from Gideon and ran to him, not caring what the others thought. My mate was back; our triad was once again complete. Blaze caught me as I threw myself into his arms, tucking his face into my neck and gripping my ass to hold me up.

"Now that's the kind of welcome home a man can get used to."

I whimpered and clung to him, legs around his hips, arms tight around his neck. "You were gone so long."

"I was, but I finished all the business I needed to." He nuzzled my neck, growling and massaging my ass at the same time. "We have three whole days to get back to Merriweather Fields and just be us."

I jerked back, my eyebrows high as I saw his smile. "Really?"

"Really?" Dante asked, looking surprised as he hurried over to wrap the two of us in his arms.

"Really. Now tell me, why are we having a party?"

I laughed and slid down his body, raising an eyebrow at him as my hips rolled over his very hard cock. He winked at me in return.

"It's no party; just the boys coming to bring me my bags so we can leave from here."

A slow grin spread across his face, his eyes bright as he looked from me to Dante. "You're all ready to leave? With us?"

"Yes." I stepped back into his arms, this time leaving my feet on the ground. "I'm ready to go whenever and wherever my mates lead me."

Blaze growled and pulled me close, his lips capturing mine in a deep kiss. Dante pressed against me from behind, nuzzling my neck.

"We'll just leave you three alone," Killian said, making the three of us jump apart. I'd almost forgotten they were there, too caught up in a moment with my mates.

Killian gave me one last hug before pulling back with a sad smile. "I love you, sis. Good travels to you, and I hope to see you all very soon."

"You're welcome at Merriweather Fields anytime, Alpha Killian. And my young friend, I see you were successful in your quest for your mate." Blaze grasped Gideon's arm in greeting, smiling when the younger shifter put an arm around his new mate.

"I did, and congratulations on finding your third. I guess the Gathering really is the place to bring fated mates together."

Blaze and Dante grinned, their obvious happiness warming my heart in ways nothing else could.

"Yes," Blaze said, glancing down at me. "It truly is."

As soon as the two couples left, my men and I settled on the couch, still holding hands, refusing to break the physical connection we'd all apparently been missing. Blaze nuzzled the side of my face and neck, leaving small kisses and nibbles along the way. The feel of his teeth in my skin made arousal flare within me, my pussy throbbing with want. Which reminded me—

"We have a little unfinished business before we're able to leave," I said as sternly as I could. Blaze stiffened in surprise, but Dante winked at me. I bit my lip and raised my eyebrow at him, to which he grinned and nodded.

"What are you two planning?" Blaze asked. I rose to my feet,

Dante doing the same. We each reached for our mate, stripping him of his business suit in a matter of seconds. Naked, sprawled on the same couch where we'd first coupled, he was the epitome of sexy. From his tousled blond hair to his blue eyes, the curve of his full lips to his lean muscles, he looked like he was meant for sex. Built for it. And I needed to test that theory. Reaching for Dante, I pulled off the T-shirt he wore and tossed it to the side. Dante did the same for me, the two of us quickly divesting each other of all the annoying clothing standing in our way.

When we were naked, I cocked a hip and gave Blaze a stern look. "There's the issue of a single mating bite left to be given."

Dante nodded. "It's absolutely something that should be corrected immediately. We can't have such an uneven coupling."

"Tripling?" I asked, scrunching my nose as I looked at him.

"Hmm, perhaps." Dante shrugged before returning his gaze to a very amused-looking Blaze. "Besides, I've now been inside our darling new mate's pussy four times, and you've yet to experience the joy. I think it's time to even the score."

"I am feeling awfully empty." I gave Blaze a pout as I straddled him, holding my hips off his lap so as not to give his dick a bit of attention. "And really needy."

Blaze growled and lifted his hips, but I shook my head. He tried to kiss me, but I pulled back. Smiling. Letting him know I was teasing him. Finally, after the third try to pull me down on his lap, Dante reached between us, gripping Blaze's dick and sliding it back and forth along my pussy. I sighed and watched, loving the way his brown skin contrasted with the deep pink of Blaze's dick. Shivering when Dante pressed the head against my clit on an upward pass.

"My mate needs me?" Blaze asked, his voice a rough whisper.

I nodded, widening my eyes for effect. "I'm just so wet for you, my darling Blasius." I leaned into his hold, rubbing my breasts against his chest and moving my lips closer to his ear. "I've been dreaming of your dick sliding inside of me since I watched Dante blow you last night."

Blaze growled as he yanked me closer, capturing my lips with his. I lifted up enough so Dante could press Blaze's dick against my opening before sliding down with a groan. Damn, he felt good. Longer than Dante but not quite as thick, he touched places inside that had never been touched. Went deeper than any other. I rocked and spread my legs wider, wanting even more, loving the way he filled me so completely. His hands gripped my ass, keeping me moving at the pace he chose, making me follow his lead. Not that I minded.

Dante sat beside us, legs spread wide, his hand tugging on his dick as he watched.

"She's tight, isn't she?" he asked, groaning as he teased the tip. Blaze growled and nodded, his fingers clawing at my bare back and his hips pumping under me.

"Fuck, yes. Tight and hot. So hot."

"It's your turn, baby," I whispered against his mouth as he whined and moaned and jerked his hips faster. I knew he needed to come, knew he wanted it as much as I did. "Let me claim you, Blaze. I'm yours, and I want you to be mine."

Blaze roared, dropping his head back just enough to expose his neck. "Yes, fuck, yes. Please."

I licked the spot I'd chosen for him, high on his neck so it could be seen even above the pressed dress shirts he wore. To hell with propriety; I wanted the entire world to see my mark on him. Know he was owned. Claimed.

And as he pressed deeper, hands on my ass and head thrown back, I bit him, making his orgasm crest, bringing on my own as I writhed in his lap. Dante came with a grunt, shooting streams across his stomach as his eyes locked on mine. The three of us still connected, coming together as our triad was finally, irrevocably, sealed.

When Dante finished, he sat up and wrapped the two of us in his arms, cuddling us together. And though I knew things would be hard, that Blaze's position and responsibilities would leave Dante and me to bear the pain of loneliness time and again, I also knew my men were worth it.

The fates had blessed me more than I could have ever dreamed possible, had smiled down on me in ways I'd never imagined.

Sweaty, sated, and happier than I'd ever been, I sent up a quick thanks to the gods for bringing us together. For forcing Killian to join the NALB. And for leading us to the Gathering.

Coming Home

blasius, dante & moira

Chapter One

moira

"Oh my God, it's huge."

"I do so love it when you say that, Moira." Dante dropped my suitcase on the marble floor, the sound echoing through the vast hallway.

I rolled my eyes as Blaze chuckled. They'd both been nearly giddy in the helicopter on the flight to Chicago. Not that I could blame them. With our bonding complete, the three of us joined forever in a triad mating, I was feeling a little giddy myself. Meeting Dante and Blaze, two wolf shifters who'd been mated to each other for nearly five centuries, had irrevocably changed my life. I went from being a single shewolf in a small pack in the Appalachians to one-third of the most powerful triad in all of North American wolf shifters.

As president of the National Association of the Lycan Brotherhood, Blaze, or Blasius Zenne, was the leader of the wolf shifter community, a title he took seriously. And Dante, as his mate, had made himself well-known as well by running the private security and investigative forces Blaze employed.

Learning I'd been chosen by the fates as their balanced third, the final addition to complete the very rare triad union, had been an amazing experience. They made me feel stronger, useful, and needed.

That was, until I walked into the palace the two of them apparently called home. Suddenly, the cotton dress I'd thought would be cute to travel in seemed way too casual, and the simplicity of my life before my mating seemed to almost dirty the gaudy grandeur around me. Mountain cabin to city mansion within forty-eight hours… It was all a bit much.

"What's the plan for today?" Blaze asked, adorably casual in faded jeans and a black T-shirt. How he didn't feel underdressed in this ridiculous foyer was beyond me. There was a chandelier, for crying out loud! A big, bright, crystal-encrusted chandelier with brass chains hanging it from the high ceiling. It probably cost more than all the cars my pack owned.

No, not my pack. Not any longer. Former pack…a thought that made my stomach drop out. I'd had to leave my pack and family behind to follow my mates to Merriweather Fields, the home of the president of the NALB. My home now.

"Well, my love," Dante said, his smile falling as his dark eyes met mine. "I believe you and Moira here will have an afternoon to yourselves."

"What?" I asked, spinning so fast my dark hair flew out around me like a cape. "Why? I thought we had three days to ourselves before work resumed." Ugh, I hated to sound whiny, but I already felt completely off-kilter. I'd grown up on the side of a mountain with only my pack around me. When we'd agreed to join the NALB so we could attend their annual social event in hope of bringing mates back with us, no one could have known the zigzag my life would take. I went from being the sister of a small pack's Alpha to the mate of the leader of our shifter community in a moment. There hadn't been a lot of processing time yet, and I wasn't ready for my mates to leave me alone in this place. The halls were too big, the ceilings too high, and that damn chandelier looked as if it had teeth.

"I'm sorry," Dante said, stepping toward me, slow and wary. "There's an issue I need the staff to address. It won't take me too long, and then I'll be right back for a little quiet time with both my gorgeous mates." He pulled me into his arms, warming me, making me feel grounded in the strange space. The space filled with staff…they had staff…I now had staff. Oh hell. "I promise, let me deal with this one thing then I'm yours for the whole three days we get to keep Blaze to ourselves."

I frowned for a moment, but Dante swooped in and brought my bottom lip between his, sucking on it and making me moan. I opened my mouth to him, kissing him at a slow, wet pace that made my heart race. Damn, I needed my men. It'd only been a few hours since I'd groaned through an orgasm, coming around Dante's talented tongue as Blaze rode him from behind. A few hours…nothing, really…and yet, the desperation for my mates clawed at me. Made me clingy and aroused. Needy in a nonsensical sort of way.

Dante pulled back slowly, licking his lips, his eyes dark and his lids heavy. "I think Blaze should take over, dove."

I nodded, sighing as the man in question pressed himself against my back. At least I wasn't being left alone just yet. I wasn't ready for that. Blaze leaned over my shoulder to give Dante a quick kiss goodbye and then set to work stripping my dress from my body.

"Aren't you going to show me the bedroom?" I asked. Blaze's hands rubbed hot and rough against my skin in a way that made me practically purr with delight.

Blaze shook his head against my shoulder before biting my neck. Hard. I jerked and growled, melting back into his hold as his tongue soothed that sting. His hands kept exploring, running all over my bare body. My hips, my waist, lifting my breasts, pinching my nipples. All the while, he kept his mouth on my neck, licking me, biting me. Driving me absolutely crazy.

"We don't need a bedroom, sweet girl. We don't need a bed or a couch or even a rug. Hell, I could take you right here in the foyer. Press you up against that wall and fill your sweet pussy from behind."

I shivered, imagining his dirty words playing out, how hot he'd feel against my back. How strong he'd be. How good he'd stretch me as he slid into my swollen pussy. Already, I could feel the trickle down my thighs as his fingers played with me, teasing me, touching soft and slow.

"You like that thought, don't you?" Blaze asked. He pushed me forward until I was pressed against the wall, my hands coming up on either side of my head, palms flat. "You like the idea of my taking control. Deciding what we do and where. How fast I enter you and how deep I thrust."

I growled, unable to help myself. "Yes."

"Hmmm, I wouldn't have expected that so soon, sweet girl. You've been so dominating to both Dante and me, demanding exactly what you wanted and how." He pressed himself against me, his body so hard and strong as it owned mine. "Not that I don't like your will, Moira. I do. I like everything about you. It doesn't matter who's on top; we'll both win. Multiple times, if I get my way."

I twisted enough to look back at him, wanting to make a sarcastic remark about winning, but that damned chandelier caught my attention before I could find his eyes. Glittering, shining, smiling with its crystal-tipped teeth, mocking me. I tried to shake off the distraction, to refocus on my mate's hands and teeth and tongue, but Blaze must have noticed. He pulled away to give me room, his breaths coming in pants and his hands holding me to him more gently than before. Giving me an out if I needed one.

"What's wrong?"

I shook my head, unable to catch my breath. "Nothing."

He spun me and crouched lower, lifting my chin with one gentle finger until I was forced to meet his gaze. "Something happened there to make you go so rigid. Tell me."

I shook my head and tried to pull him to me, needing his comfort, feeling overly exposed all of a sudden. He took a step back, refusing me. My stomach plummeted and the earth tilted as everything screeched to a halt.

"You don't want me?"

Blaze sighed and pulled me into his arms. "Of course I want you. Every second of every day, no matter where I am or who I'm with, I want you. Your smile, your deep eyes, your wit, your strength—I want it all, every inch of it." He leaned down, licking the seam of my lips with a growl. "I want your pussy on my face and your hands around my cock. I want you in every way, every position, in control or submissive as hell. I don't care who takes the reins in our intimacies, I just want to drown myself in you. But this—" he looked me up and down, his brow furrowed "—this doesn't seem like you. Moira O'Shea walked into the council room with the president of the NALB and ruled it without saying a word, above and beyond your own Alpha, who's no weakling by any stretch. You demanded a joint claiming, both of us inside of you at once, when Dante and I would have happily settled for one at a time to keep from hurting you. Moira O'Shea climbed into my lap and took what she needed, sexually and emotionally, and bravely came home with two new mates and no knowledge of what lay ahead of her. My sweet girl could take on the world, and I'd happily sit back and let her. Right now, though, you're literally trembling in my arms, and not because of my kisses." He frowned, eyebrows drawn together. "What's wrong, Moira?"

I shook my head again, keeping my eyes down, trying hard not to stare at the fucking chandelier. Not to notice the marble on the floor or the exotic wood on the walls. Searching for something to cling to as the world spun away from me.

Blaze sighed, his displeasure obvious, which only made me feel worse. "Talk to me, mate."

I closed my eyes, clawing at him, needing his strength.

"Can we—" I licked my lips and clung to his shirt as I opened my eyes and peered up at him "—move this to the bedroom? I'd feel more comfortable in a smaller space, something a bit more private."

Blaze stared down at me, his bright eyes guarded and disbelieving. I did my best to hold that powerful gaze, to prove to him I was okay. The chandelier glittered in the corner of my eye, daring me to look its way, trying to pry my attention from my mate. Stupid, scary light fixture.

Finally, Blaze sighed and nodded. "Whatever you want, my sweet girl. Whatever you need to be comfortable."

He picked up my dress and handed it to me, avoiding my eyes. I clung to the fabric, using it to shield my nudity, knowing I had just screwed up but having no idea how to fix it. I followed Blaze down the hallway, skirting the edges of the hall to walk past the chandelier.

Past and not under…damn thing would probably crash on my head if I did that.

◊ ◊ ◊

"Oh, fuck, my sweet girl. You feel so good."

I moaned as Blaze rocked against me, his heavy erection deep inside me, the pressure of his pelvis making me shudder as it pressed against my clit. Damn, he felt so good inside me. So right.

He gripped my hands, pulling them up toward the headboard, pinning me down. I arched and growled, spreading my knees wider, lifting them to his ribs to open myself to him.

"I should flip you over," he growled, keeping his face in my neck, thrusting hard at a slow pace that was driving me insane.

"Pull that ass up and fuck you until you scream. Make you beg for release as I spank that pretty ass to a lovely shade of pink. Would you like that, sweet girl?"

I shivered and mewled, but I had no time to answer him.

"Well, I certainly wouldn't mind that show."

Dante's unexpected voice had me turning my head in his direction, gasping in surprise. He smiled as he stood next to the enormous bed, watching us, his own erection obvious in his thin dress pants. Blaze had tossed me onto the massive pile of pillows as soon as we'd entered their bedroom. Dark, tall, and wide, with soft sheets and too many pillows to count, it was a bed made for loveplay. And we'd been taking advantage of it for hours.

"Care to join us?" Blaze asked, still sliding in and out of me, his pace slow and languorous. Teasing me in the best way.

"Not quite yet, my love. I'm really enjoying the view."

He smirked and licked his lips, his tongue almost obscenely slow as it travelled across the dark flesh. His view had to be quite explicit, as he'd positioned himself slightly toward the end of the bed. I could only imagine the picture: Blaze sliding in and out of my pink pussy, the flex of his ass on every push in, his balls heavy and hanging. I could feel them slap against me, knew they had to be adding to the erotic visage Dante was staring at in interest. I brought my knees even higher, tilting my hips up, opening myself to his eyes and licking my lips as he growled.

"Such a pretty picture my mates make," Dante said. He unzipped his trousers and let them fall to the floor, freeing his hard dick to my hungry view. "So very tantalizing."

He kneeled on the bed, sliding his hands over Blaze's hips and down. Down, down, to where we were joined, his fingers forming a V around Blaze's dick, pressing against me, adding an extra layer of sensation.

"Fuck." Blaze jolted, dropping his forehead against mine. "Do you like this, mate? All three of us back together in bed?"

I nodded, growling deep and low like a purr. Without warning, Blaze slid out of me, flipping me to my stomach and pulling my hips up in the air. Before I could catch my balance, he slammed back inside, pushing me up the bed and making me grunt.

"Get her to make that sound again, my love," Dante said as he slid around to lie beneath me. I stared down the length of my body, nearly coming at the view. Blaze's legs on either side of mine, pushing and flexing against me. Dante's darker skin sitting in such contrast to the pale sheets, his tightly curled hair brushing my belly as he maneuvered his way between my legs.

I licked my lips and groaned, wishing he would join us, that he'd use his fingers or his tongue on me as Blaze slammed into my pussy. I needed them both, needed them to make me feel grounded and secure. Needed them to make me feel like me.

The sensation of Dante's lips suckling my clit had me yelping and arching off the bed. He chuckled against me, increasing the pressure, making me writhe and shake as the pleasure built inside of me. Hot and wet and filled and so damn close, I stuttered, words falling from my lips without my knowledge, my body reacting to the pleasure solely on instinct. Shaking. Clinging.

Coming.

Blaze increased the pace and strength of his thrusts, making me slide up the bed on my knees as my orgasm swept over me. I cried into the pillows and clung to the sheets, my fingers fisting the soft cotton like a lifeline. Dante slid out from under me, his hand gliding up and down his own erection as he watched, coming in his hand after only a few strokes. Blaze kept thrusting, pulling me against him until he roared and held himself deep, coming inside of me with jerky hip bumps and a snarl that made me shiver.

Sticky, wet, and sated, the three of us cuddled together on the soft bedding. Catching our breaths. Reconfirming our connection.

"My beautiful loves." Dante kissed Blaze deeply as his hands slid around my hips, pulling me to lie between them. "I'm so happy we're all finally home together."

Home…the word struck me somewhere deep inside, setting off alarm bells. As I closed my eyes to rest between my mates, the memory of that damned chandelier mocked me, making me feel somehow inadequate. That light fixture was some kind of symbol for this entire mansion, which made me feel less than acceptable. The chandelier was far too grand to be in the home of a girl like me.

Chapter Two

"But there has to be something I can do."

Blaze smiled and leaned in to kiss my forehead. Normally, a move I saw as sweet. This time, it seemed condescending.

"You need to rest, sweet girl. You've obviously started going into your heat cycle, and I just want you comfortable and happy."

I crossed my arms over my chest. "And how exactly would you know I've started going into my heat?"

His eyes widened and he blinked twice. "Well, you've been a bit...not yourself."

I raised an eyebrow and waited.

Blaze fidgeted with the ends of his tie, something I'd never seen him do before. "You've seemed so tired, and your mood has put both Dante and me on edge."

"Don't bring me into this," Dante said, sweeping me into a hug. "Do whatever you want to do today, my dove. And I see nothing wrong with your mood."

"Not helping, Dante," Blaze growled, glowering at the

smaller man.

Dante chuckled and pressed his lips to mine, giving me the softest, briefest kiss. "Don't be too hard on him. He knows not how wrong he is to comment on such things."

"So basically, you agree with him but don't want to get in trouble by saying so?" I took a step back, glaring at my idiot mates. They turned to stare at one another, neither saying a word. I huffed a big sigh and shook my head. "Get out. Go to work. Be productive and needed. I'll be sitting here doing nothing."

I spun and hurried back to the bedroom before either man could stop me. Damn it, my emotions *were* all over the place. Maybe I was about to go into heat. I'd never had a problem in the past with mood swings, but I was mated now. Things were different.

Everything was different.

I tossed myself on the bed, but the sleep I strived for refused to come. Every time I came close to dropping off, that damned chandelier in the main foyer would swing into my thoughts and startle me awake. The thing seemed to be out for me, which was why I'd hardly left the bedroom in days. That, and my mates had kept me quite occupied while we all enjoyed Blaze's time off. But the minivacation was over, and the boys were headed back out into the mansion to work. Meanwhile, I stayed behind with nothing to do, nowhere to go, and a giant chandelier making me feel smaller by the hour.

Such a ridiculous thing to be afraid of.

After too long lying in bed not sleeping, I threw off the covers and stalked into the bathroom. I needed a break. I needed to release some tension. I needed to explore this ridiculous palace instead of hiding in the back of the private wing like a coward.

Fifteen minutes later, I was dressed, polished, and ready to go. Sadly, I was also standing in the foyer staring at that gaudy chandelier.

"Just…walk under it," I said, suddenly so thankful none of Blaze's guards stayed in the personal wing. They'd truly think I was off my rocker if they heard me talking to myself, especially about a light fixture.

I took a deep breath, lifted my chin…

And scurried along the wall so as not to walk directly underneath the ridiculous thing.

When I reached the main doors to the mansion, I paused, unsure what to do. Blaze and Dante had guards in place out there. There was a retinal scanner, for Pete's sake! If I left, would I be able to get back in? Would the guards know who I was or think I was a threat? I'd been in Merriweather Fields for four days, and I had yet to leave the private wing. I had a brief niggle of "maybe you should wait for one of your mates" before I huffed and stomped to the door. Screw it… I'd never been afraid to walk down a hallway before, why start now?

I swung open the door, only to find a huge shifter staring at me, wide-eyed.

"Miss Moira," he said, seeming nervous. "Is there something I can do for you?"

I faltered, unsure of protocol. "Uh…no, I'm just going for a walk."

"A walk?" he asked. "Is the president aware of your plans?"

I stood taller, his words making something buried deep under new fears bristle. "Is there some reason I can't go for a walk?"

"No, ma'am. It's just—" He looked around as if searching for help. "Ma'am, President Zenne was adamant that you were not going to be leaving the private wing."

"Well, President Zenne was wrong. I'm going for a walk."

He cursed as I walked away, though he didn't follow me. Small victory, I assumed. But the farther away from the private wing I walked, the more I realized how little I had actually won. Guards popped up at every corner, watching me, staring with their almost identical flat eyes. The farther I walked, the worse it got. Finally, I snuck through a set of double doors, slamming them behind me and leaning against them with my eyes closed, just to get a break from the constant pressure of their eyes on me.

When I reopened my eyes, my jaw dropped. Books. From the floor to the soaring ceiling above, lining every wall. All colors and sizes, they created a painting within the dark wood shelves where they rested. Over the tall windows, stacked on tables, piled on the huge desk, books owned this room. I loved it.

"Dove?" Dante's voice was soft, careful, as he walked through a door on the far side of the room. "What are you doing down here?"

"I—" I paused and licked my lips, still intrigued by all the information housed in the room, "—I wanted to walk around."

"We could take you for a tour after work, if you like."

I shook my head, staring at a wall of green leather spines. "I'm fine on my own."

The leather felt cold under my fingers, rough with age. I trailed a finger along the top edge, reading titles when I could, wondering about the different languages some were written in when I couldn't.

"You like to read?" Dante asked. I glanced over my shoulder, smiling at him.

"Very much so."

He moved to the desk, resting a hip on the corner and crossing his legs at the ankles. "This is Blaze's personal library. Five hundred years of knowledge, all hoarded away by one man."

"Just Blaze?"

Dante hummed, moving closer. "Yes. It's his one obsession, the thing most of his income goes to. These books encompass years of his hard work and make up the majority of his wealth."

I yanked my fingers away from the leather, the unknown value of such a collection making me uneasy even as my eyes skittered across title after title. "It's incredibly beautiful."

"So are you."

I grinned and snuck a peek at him over my shoulder. "You're biased."

"Not in the least. Every man in this building would say the same." He approached slowly, stalking me, very much making me his prey. "The guards are all whispering about you, did you know?"

"I assumed." My breath caught as he pressed himself against my back, the warmth of his body making me tingle.

"They can smell Blaze and me on you, and they're curious about our loveplay. A beautiful, sexy shifter joining an established mating. It's the stuff men dream about."

I sighed as his hands slid up to cover my breasts. "Not just men."

He chuckled against my neck as his fingers pinched and teased my nipples. "What do you dream of, my dove? What fantasies do you have that we haven't learned?" He growled, biting my neck, massaging my heavy breasts, and pressing his erection against my ass. "What thought makes those fingers of yours bury themselves deep inside your sweet pussy?"

I dropped my forehead against the bookcase, breathing hard, wetness spreading between my legs.

"I don't…" I stumbled over my words, unsure, shaking my head. "I don't know."

His fingers paused, and he pulled his head back from my neck. "You don't know?"

"No."

He slid his hand down my stomach, lower, cupping my pussy over the fabric of my dress. "That doesn't sound like you."

"What?" I writhed against his hand, desperate. Needy. Wanting.

He leaned harder against me, pushing me into the bookcase as his fingers began a wicked massage over my swollen clit.

"You're so confident, so sure. You climbed on top of the most powerful shifter who's ever lived and demanded he claim you the way you wanted to be claimed. I would have expected you to give me a list of your desires in order of priority with full details of places and possibilities, not tell me you don't know."

Pressing harder, his fingers brought me higher and higher toward my orgasm, teasing and stroking and working me in just the right way. And God, I loved it. Loved the feel of him rutting against me, loved the way he dominated me, loved how he was so focused on my pleasure.

Oh fuck, I loved *him*. Something I hadn't said, hadn't truly thought about. Hadn't given myself the chance to realize.

"Dante." My orgasm stole my breath, leaving his name with little more than a rough growl behind it. He continued his torment, rubbing me through my clothes, teasing me through my pleasure. Making it last. Making me nearly weak with the power of it.

"Did you like that, dove?" he growled, still hard, still pressing against my ass.

"Yes."

"Good." He pulled back. I waited for him to pull up my skirt, to grab my hips and press inside me, but instead he pulled the fabric down so it fluttered around my knees and turned me to face him.

"I have to go back to work, my dove. You think about those fantasies; I want you to tell me all about them tonight."

"What about you?"

"What about me?"

I trailed a single fingertip over the obvious erection behind his suit pants. "What about this?"

He chuckled. "I'll deal with it. There isn't time to do all the delicious things I want to with you right now, and I am a man who never does anything half-assed."

Dante leaned down, kissing the pout off my lips. His dark

eyes speared me, saying so much without words.

"Are you going back to the private wing?" he asked, holding me in his arms, rocking me as I clung to him.

I shrugged. "I was thinking of finding the kitchen. I'm hungry."

"The staff will bring you food."

And just like that, my happy afterglow mood fell. Chandeliers and staff who brought me food. Just…no.

I shook my head against his chest. "I like to cook."

He pulled back, watching me, his face concerned. "Are you sure you're okay?"

"I'm fine," I huffed. "I just want to make my own lunch, if that's allowed."

His dark eyebrows rose. "We're not lording over you, Moira. You have no rules here."

"But the guards—"

"The guards are here to keep you safe, not contain you. If you want to go for a walk, go. If you want to shift and go for a run, please do. But take a guard with you. You are precious and vital to Blaze and me. We want you safe."

I sighed, feeling guilty and ridiculous. My mates had waited centuries to find me, their missing third. Of course they were only concerned about my safety. "I know."

"Go, cook some food if that's what you want to do." He pulled back after one final kiss. "You'll find the kitchens in the basement."

I stared at him, at his choice of word. Hoping I misheard him. "Kitchens?"

He shrugged, casual, as if having multiple kitchens was somehow normal. "We have a lot of people here to feed." He gave me a sad smile and pulled free from my hold. "I really must get back to work. Is there anything else you need?"

"No, I'm good." I wrapped my arms around my chest, chilled and altogether uncomfortable. "You go on."

"Moira, are you—"

"Really. I'm fine," I interrupted, the burn of growing tears making me rush. Wishing he would just leave. "I'll go find the kitchens. Plural."

His eyebrows fell, a look of worry and sadness crossing his handsome face. "If you're sure."

"Go, you silly man." I pasted on my brightest smile and waved. "I'm fine."

He nodded once, whispering, "Have fun, my dove," before turning away. Dante left out the side door with a blown kiss, one final look back before he left me alone. As soon as the door closed behind him, the smile dropped from my face and I curled my shoulders inward. Sadness and confusion made my heart hurt and my stomach twist. What was I here? Who was I here? Just the mate of the owners? The weak link in their life, locked away in a far-off wing, kept separate from the rest of the shifters who came and went through the mansion? And if so, how would that ever be enough? How could I ever be enough for them if I could barely leave the private wing?

Giving the library one final, covetous look, I hurried to the door and strode out into the hallway.

"Ma'am." A guard nodded at me from his post across the hall. "I've been asked to show you to the kitchens."

I shook my head. "No, I'm going back to the private wing."

"Oh." He looked confused. "I thought Mister Dante said—"

"It doesn't matter what Mister Dante said," I yelled. Closing my eyes, I reined in my temper and pursed my lips. "I'm not going to the kitchens. I just…want to go back to bed."

CHAPTER THREE

moira

I awoke one morning to find the bed on fire. Not literally, though by the way my bones hurt and my skin burned, it sure seemed like it. My heat cycle had begun, just as Blaze had thought it would. And oh, did it make me ache for the touch of my mates.

"Dante? Blaze?" I rolled, groaning, reaching for my mates. All I could find was an empty bed and cold sheets. They'd left.

Not that I blamed them.

I'd barely touched either of them the past few days, my uncomfortableness in my new home tearing apart the physical bond we all shared. I knew it—I think deep down they knew it—but none of us talked about it. They simply watched me, waiting and wary, as they went about their days. And I…I hid in the bedroom.

But today would have to be different.

I crawled out of bed and lurched to the bathroom. A cold shower would help, at least for a few minutes. Long enough for me to find one of my mates. And it did help, the icy spray clearing my head enough to make my plans. Get dressed, roam the halls, find Dante or Blaze, and have them help me the way only they could. With sex and orgasms and the touch of the men fated as mine. My heat was on, and there was no way I could hope to curtail the pain without the assistance of my mates.

Once dressed in the softest, loosest item I owned—a cheery yellow sundress that looked far happier than I felt—I shuffled off to find my mates. That damned chandelier mocked me, making me nervous, but I couldn't wait or let it stop me. My heat would devour me, burn me alive from the inside out if I didn't find my men.

With little more than a panicked glance up, I stalked down the hall, right under the ugly light. An accomplishment that would have had me grinning on any other day. When I reached the doors to the main hall, I threw them open so forcefully, they slammed into the wall behind them and made the guard spin in shock.

"Ma'am, can I help…" He sniffed. Sniffed again, and then his eyes went dark. Pupils wide, he stared at me, a low growl rumbling through his chest. The sound of a shifter aroused.

"They'll kill you if you even think of it." I tossed my head and hurried down the hall, refusing to let my nervousness show. Damn it. Every man in this building would be able to smell my heat on me. There was no way to hide it or cover it with perfume. My cycle, the one time every year a shewolf was fertile and ready to mate, hadn't slowly crept over me like in the past. No, this one had come on overnight, giving me no time to prepare or to ready my mates for my needs. Not that they wouldn't already know what my oncoming heat cycle meant; hell, they were probably excited for it. Every shifter knew a shewolf in heat needed sex, and lots of it. It was what nature wanted, the only time we were able to reproduce. Our hormones would rage for days, the heat burning us alive, unless our mate sated our needs, preferably with his or her or their, in my case, body.

Really, it should have been a wonderful, glorious time filled with orgasms and emotions and all kinds of sensual kinkery. A time to grow closer: physically, emotionally, and intimately. It was why the Gathering was held in December, so new mates could spend their winter heat cycle sectioned off from the rest of their packs, getting to know one another, and if lucky, falling in love. Instead, my heat started while I was alone, too confused and preoccupied with my ridiculous obsession of proper place and station and wealth to pay attention to my body, and my mates were somewhere in this maze of a mansion with fifty men between them and me. Not the ideal situation.

I skirted the guards as best I could, but I couldn't avoid them entirely. I felt their eyes on me, sensed more than heard their desirous growls. A shewolf in heat could tear a pack apart if the unmated males had nowhere to direct their energy. It was why most mates hunkered down in a private den during the shewolf's heat cycle. Why unmated females tended to grab a partner early in the season and run off for a few days of alone time before the cycle began. But no, not my triad. Not me. Not this time. My heat would have to be suffered in public, at least until I found Dante and Blaze.

Slipping into the library, I spun, hope a rapidly filling balloon in my chest. Sadly, my balloon deflated quickly, the room sitting silent and empty. Determined, I crossed to the door Dante had used a few days before, crossing my fingers I'd find him. Instead, I found another hallway, much like the last. Sighing, I slipped out and continued my hunt, scenting the air and trying my damnedest to pinpoint my mates. Even my mating bond to them wasn't as helpful as I'd hoped, or the hallways and rooms were too convoluted for me to get a good feel for where they were. Either way, I suffered through a sense of loss, my gut roiling as the temperature under my skin increased, unable to find my quarry.

After walking down endless hallways and making an untold

number of turns, I approached an open door and heard Blaze laugh. My knees went weak at the knowledge I'd found him, and I sagged against the wall. As my joints popped and my muscles simmered, he laughed again. I closed my eyes, leaning my head against the wall. God, the sound of that man happy was perfect. All deep and throaty and full—a real man's laugh. Sexy. It made me want to growl and stalk him, rub myself against him and beg him to touch me. And I would have—I even approached the door, ready to walk in—except an older gentleman, one in an official-looking robe, sat with my mate. Talking. Papers scattered on the table before them. My heart sank and I sagged against the wall once more.

Meetings…always with the meetings.

I stood in the shadows across the hall, watching, waiting for my chance, wishing Blaze would notice me so I wouldn't have to interrupt something that could be very important. Feeling less and less sure of myself as the minutes passed, as he neglected to notice me. As I stood alone and in pain and needful.

"He'll pick taking care of your needs over that old blowhard, you know," a man said. Before I could turn, he pressed himself against my back, holding me to him as he whispered in my ear, "A mate in heat is a male's first priority. You should go in there."

I shook my head. "I can't."

"Why not?"

I licked my lips, my voice coming out softer than planned. "I don't want to interrupt him."

The man stepped back, chuckling. "You wouldn't have to say a word. He'd smell it before you even crossed the threshold. Just approach the door, and he'll rush you back to your private wing to temper that burn."

I closed my eyes for a moment, swallowing hard as the heat inside of me intensified. Every inch of my skin felt tight, squeezing me, adding to the deluge of agony that grew with every moment I stood in that hall. But the idea of Blaze ignoring me or turning me away hurt worse, and so I waited. Alone. Well, not quite alone.

When I opened my eyes, the man stood in front of me, watching. Huge, with big muscles and dark tattoos peeking out from under his shirt, he stared at me with a glint in his blue eyes. Eyes I'd never seen before.

"Who are you?" I asked.

He shrugged. "I'm just a worker bee."

"How do you know who I am, who he is to me?"

He chuckled again, a rough, masculine sound. "Moira O'Shea, every wolf on this continent knows who you are."

I took a step back, my face tightening as I frowned. "Why?"

"Because you're the only woman able to tame two of the strongest Alphas to ever live. No one believed they'd find their third. How rare is a woman with enough courage to make demands of Blasius and stand up to Dante? How strong of will must such a woman be?" He cocked his head, appraising. "Though perhaps we're wrong. Perhaps you're not as commanding as everyone expects."

I glanced from him to where Blaze sat just beyond the open doors leading into the room. I wanted my mate so badly, needed to feel his skin on mine, his taste on my lips. And yet…

"I don't know where I fit in this place," I whispered, the words surprising me. The stranger shrugged.

"You fit with them. All this—" he waved his hand around, indicating the mansion "—it's a facade to impress outsiders like that guy talking to Blaze. It's not who they are or you are. Stage dressing, Miss Moira." He leaned close, his lips brushing my ear, his arms wrapping around me in a strange sort of hug. "You're the star."

Before I could respond, he let me go and spun toward the open door. "But if you're too afraid to tell your mate you need him, I'll do it for you."

He winked over his shoulder and approached the door.

My heart nearly stopped as the icy cold reality of what had just happened washed over me. The talking, the touching, the hug… He carried my scent on him. A strange man, unmated, I had to assume, was about to walk into a room with my mate, smelling of me. Of my heat.

I lurched forward. "Wait."

Blaze's growl interrupted my call and forced me back a step, overpowering in both volume and force. My mate went from proper businessman to raging street fighter in under a second, leaping from the chair across the room to grab the stranger by the shoulders and shove him backward.

"Where's Moira?" Blaze snarled, his eyes glowing with the spirit of his wolf.

The stranger shrugged, remarkably casual in the face of such a warrior. "Don't you know?"

Blaze's lip curled up, his eyes lifting at the corners as he began to shift. As he lost control of his wolf. "Jameson, if you did anything—"

"I'm here." I stepped across the threshold—the draw to be with my mate, to calm him, to keep him from destroying his image as a serious leader, too hard to resist. "I'm fine, and I'm right here."

Blaze shoved Jameson out of his way, knocking the man to the ground as he rushed to me. His eyes ran all over my body, inspecting me, darkening as they took me in.

"You're in heat."

I nodded, unable to speak as his growl rumbled low in his chest. Jesus, the way his eyes looked at me…devoured me. He looked like a man possessed, and I was quite obviously his salvation.

The older shifter coughed. "President Zenne, I do believe—"

"Someone will call to reschedule our meeting, Ignacious. I have something pressing to take care of."

Blaze grabbed my elbow and dragged me from the room,

leaving behind an affronted Ignacious and a chuckling Jameson.

"Blaze, really," I said, keeping my voice soft and quiet. "You could have finished your meeting. I was trying not to interrupt you."

"Are you in pain?" he asked. The anger in his tone made my step falter, my heart jump, but I still answered honestly.

"Yes," I whispered.

"I thought so." Blaze threw open the doors to the library, dragging me into the room and locking them behind us. "Get on the desk."

I took a step back. "Excuse me?"

"You're in heat, which is causing you pain. You need someone to bring you to orgasm to ease that burn. Get your ass on that desk and spread your legs so I can take care of you."

"Take care of me?" I took another step back, this one to keep from hitting him. "Is that what I am already? A problem for you to fix?"

"Damn it, Moira. That's not what I said."

"No, but it's your intention. Take care of the problem and go back to work."

"No." His growl blasted through the room. It should have scared me, made me cower. But I was quickly becoming sick of cowering.

"Really?" I stepped toward him, head up, challenging. "So now I don't understand your words, is that it? Are you sure you know what you meant, Blasius?"

"Yes, I'm fucking sure." He grabbed me by both arms and led me to the desk. "You are my top priority, though you seem to not want to be. You've been hiding from us, acting like some scared little girl. Well, if that's how you want to act, that's how I'll treat you."

He picked me up and sat me on the desk, hard. I fell back, landing on my elbows. "Blaze—"

"Spread your legs, Moira. Now."

Haltingly, while letting out a snarl of irritation, I did as I was told.

"Do you want me, mate?" he asked, a certain tone of worry creeping into his voice as he watched me. "Do you want my touch and attention?"

I swallowed hard, bitter tears building in the corners of my eyes. Damn this man and his sweetness. That tone, that uncertainty in his voice, wrecked me. He couldn't be that way in public, could only show that in private with his mates. I hadn't known him long, had really only just met him, but I knew that. I knew he lived a life of lies and window dressing.

Window dressing…like the mansion. Like Jameson had tried to tell me.

Just like that, the pressure and the stress of the last few days evaporated, leaving me feeling more like myself. Like my very aroused, needy self, lying across a desk, spreading my legs for my handsome mate. My mate who was just a man, a wolf shifter, like the rest of us. Even if his job belied that fact.

Nodding, I let my knees fall farther, opening myself to him more as I murmured a quiet, "Of course."

With nothing more than a grunt, Blaze fell to his knees and ripped my panties down my legs, tossing them to the side. He attacked my pussy without delay, his tongue finding me swollen and slick for him, his hands rough against my thighs. Growling, making me twist and whine, he yanked me across the desk, shoving my legs over his shoulders and pressing my knees toward my chest. Giving me no chance of escape. Owning me. Devouring me.

"Blaze…fuck." My head hit the desk as his fingers plunged inside. No warning, no teasing strokes. Just the delicious stretch and burn of his hand joining his mouth. He filled me from the start, curling and stroking and thrusting until I lay chanting his name, gripping his hair, and pulling him harder against me. Needing him with a desperation I couldn't express.

The orgasm Blaze demanded from my body hit suddenly, every muscle clenching as my nerve endings seemed to spark all at once. I gasped and groaned my way through it, arching hard, my heels pressing into Blaze's shoulders.

Before I could come down, before my muscles relaxed and my body stopped shuddering, Blaze flipped me to my stomach and shoved me forward. My upper body rested on top of the desk, hips at the edge, legs hanging.

"One down," he said as he slammed himself deep inside me. The force of his thrust slid the desk across the floor and lifted me to my toes. My arms flailed to the side for something to hold on to, gripping the edge of the desk, and knocking over a stack of old, leather-bound books.

"Shit, sorry." I pushed onto my palms, but Blaze grabbed my neck and held me down.

"I'm fucking you. My cock is right—" a hard thrust slid the whole desk forward another few inches "—there inside you, and you're worried about a few books?"

"I…damn it." I bit my lip and closed my eyes as his hips hit my ass again and again. The pleasure and pressure built as he hit places deep inside of me, making words hard to find. "They seem…expensive. Important."

Blaze laughed, kicking my feet wider and pulling up my hips for an even deeper angle. Oh God, he was going to kill me with this position. The pleasure would rip me apart, and I loved it. I pushed back, meeting him on every thrust. Ready to fall to pieces at his hands.

"They're nothing compared to you, my sweet girl," he said, voice deep and a growl underlying the words. "You are the treasure in this kingdom, and the sooner you learn that, the better."

He smacked my ass, the jolt of pleasure mixed with pain making me jump. I tried to turn, needing to face him, but he held me down.

"Please," I groaned, my fingers scrabbling along the slick, wooden surface. "Let me up."

"Why? You've been happy to play the submissive shewolf since we arrived here. I'm giving you what you want, aren't I?"

"Yes, but…" I grunted on a particularly deep thrust, my mind foggy with lust, my words overruled by the sound of his skin hitting mine.

"But what?"

"I…" I shivered, desperate, something circling just on the edge of my mind, barely out of reach. Something important. "I don't know."

"Yes, you do." Harder, faster, he thrust into me, making me need to come so badly, I trembled. Every inch of me owned by him. Every desire belonging only to him. He slid one hand underneath my hips, his hand cupping my pussy, teasing me but refusing to give me what I needed to get off. Forcing me to ride the edge of orgasm.

"Blaze, please," I cried, too far gone to be ashamed of begging.

"What? What do you need, sweet girl?"

One more hard thrust that sent the desk skittering across the wood floor and the wispy thoughts dancing at the edge of my mind exploded. This was what I wanted, what I needed. A deep connection to my mates, to know them and let them know me, was all that mattered. Wherever we lived or what the accommodations were like, they didn't override the base of our triad. We were a unit. Three people bound together by fate. No one and nothing, especially not some insecurities about snobby decorations, could tear us apart. We were the foundation; everything else was just window dressing.

"Fuck, Blaze." I shoved back, knocking him off-balance and forcing him out of my body. Growling, I spun and pushed him down, the two of us falling to the floor. "I need you like this."

I devoured his mouth in a brutal kiss, bruising and

demanding. Taking. Before he could say a word, I straddled his hips and slid down over him, fitting him back inside me, impaling myself with his hard cock. This time, on my terms.

"Moira," he groaned as I lifted, almost pulling myself off him, before dropping back down. He grabbed my hips, and I dropped a hand between my legs, circling my clit, bringing the other to my breast to pinch my nipple. Teasing…pushing myself harder and faster toward release. He watched me, snarling and growling and bucking as he lay on the floor. Wanting control, but letting me take it. Letting me own him for a moment.

"Fuck, you feel so good." Bouncing on his thick cock, I rocked and rotated my hips, teasing myself as much as him, driving us both toward the goal. He groaned when I reached behind me to grab his balls, massaging them, tugging just hard enough to make him shiver.

He closed his eyes and let go, allowing me the control I craved. Surrendering. I loved him like this…all out of control and driven by sensation. Loved it when he gave himself to me so fully. I took that trust seriously, made sure I gave him everything I had to show how much I appreciated it. How much it turned me on.

With a pinch to my clit and a roll of my hips, my body seized around Blaze's dick. Shaking, sweating, shouting his name as he roared. Blaze followed me, his hands gripping my hips, holding himself deep inside of me as he arched up. The orgasm calmed the crazed need my heat had brought on, eased the pain and the burn. At least for the moment.

Breathless, my head on his chest as I recovered from the exertion of riding him, I sighed and said the only words I could think of. "I hate the chandelier in the foyer."

Blaze's hands stopped their roaming, and he lifted his head off the floor. "What?"

"The chandelier. It's too…ritzy. It makes me feel somehow unworthy to be here." I sighed and waved my hand. "This whole place is very…"

"Overwhelming." He gave me a soft smile, one that demanded I press my lips to his and kiss it off his face. So I did.

I smiled when I released his lips. "Yes."

Blaze pushed my dark hair off my face, staring up at me. "Why didn't you tell me?"

"I figured I'd get used to it."

"But you didn't."

"No." I shook my head, clinging to him, my hands clutching at his shirt, somehow afraid he might leave as I admitted my ridiculous fears. "Every day, the insecurity kept getting worse. It's too much."

"So we take it down."

I pushed myself up higher. "What?"

Blaze chuckled, grabbing my arms and rolling me underneath him. "It's a goddamn light fixture, Moira. It means nothing."

"But this is your home."

"No, this is the home of the president of the NALB, which I happen to be for the moment. This isn't me, nor do I want it to be." He leaned down and bit my lower lip, making me moan. "I have homes all over the world, sweet girl. From cabins in the woods to chalets on the top of mountains. We'll find one that suits you, and that's where Dante, you, and I will go once this is all over."

"I never thought…" I whispered, unable to finish my thought due to the tears falling from my eyes. "I'm sorry, I should have said something."

Blaze ran a finger over my cheek. "You did. It just took you a few days."

Looking up at him, at this wonderful man I was blessed to have met, I whispered the only thing I had left to admit. "I love you, Blasius Zenne."

His eyes sparkled, and he grinned the most beautiful, bright smile. "I love you too, Moira O'Shea."

"Yes, of course, I love you both as well." Dante quietly shut the door behind himself, walking over with a sexy, lustful smile on his face. "Especially when you're all disheveled and obviously postcoital."

"Come join us," Blaze said, holding out a hand.

Dante wasted no time, stripping off his coat and tie to pile onto the rug with us. The three of us wrapped ourselves around one another, all touching, cuddling. Connecting as mates should.

"What were you two talking about, anyway?" Dante asked as he ran his hands over my hip.

"I was telling Blaze how much I love him," I said, staring into his dark eyes. "And I love you, too, Dante."

"Oh, my dove. I've loved you since the first night I saw you." He leaned forward, kissing me, his hand sliding over Blaze's waist and pulling us together. "What brought this lovefest on?"

Blaze chuckled from his place behind me. "Well, we were talking about decorating."

Dante paused, his brows furrowing. "Decorating?"

"Yes," Blaze said with a cocky grin. "It seems Moira's not fond of the chandelier in the foyer of the private wing."

Dante shrugged. "So we take it down. What's the big deal?"

I chuckled and buried my head in his chest as Blaze laughed behind me, bright and loud and vibrant.

"What?" Dante asked. "What did I miss?"

Blaze rolled us both, lying across me and leaning over to nuzzle Dante's neck. "Nothing, really. Though our mate has obviously gone into heat. I think it's time to take her back to our bedroom, don't you?"

I shook my head, shoving him off me. "No, I want to stay here in your library. I like this room."

"You've barely wanted to leave the bedroom for days," Dante said, smiling in surprise.

I crawled over his body, straddling him as Blaze moved to

press himself to my back.

"No more wasting time worrying. I want to christen every room with you boys. Even all the kitchens."

Books by Ellis Leigh

THE FERAL BREED
Claiming His Fate
Claiming His Need
Claiming His Witch
Claiming Their Forever: A Feral Breed Anthology
Claiming His Beauty
Claiming His Fire
Claiming His desire

FERAL BREED FOLLOWINGS
Claiming His Chance
Claiming His Prize

STAND-ALONE ROMANCE
Bearly Dreaming: A Souther Shifters Kindleworld
Masterson: A Vampire Sons Story

THE DEVIL'S DIRES
Savage Surrender

About the Author

A storyteller from the time she could talk, Ellis grew up among family legends of hauntings, psychics, and love spanning decades. Those stories didn't always have the happiest of endings, so they inspired her to write about real life, real love, and the difficulties therein. From farmers to werewolves, store clerks to witches—if there's love to be found, she'll write about it. Ellis lives in the Chicago area with her husband, daughters, and two tiny fish that take up way too much of her time.

Find Ellis online at:
Website: www.ellisleigh.com
Twitter: https://twitter.com/ellis_writes
Facebook: https://www.facebook.com/ellisleighwrites